Lover, Friend and Muse

by

Carol M. Palmer

Copyright © 2008

PART ONE

Chapter 1

Diagnosis

When I came to, everything was still foggy. I knew I wasn't at home. It was too bright for my house. How had I managed to get from my house to wherever *here* was? Then the brightness became more aggressive. It hurt my eyes to try to focus through the haze of lights. Slowly, my vision returned, and I knew where I was.

"Oh, Beatrice, you're finally awake," Jesse said to me.

"Why am I in the hospital?" I asked.

"We don't know yet. We were hoping you could tell us something. When I arrived, the ambulance was already there. Your housekeeper said she heard a crash and found you on the floor unconscious," Jesse said. "Do you remember anything?"

"Not too much, really. I was carrying a tray from the kitchen, and then, all of a sudden, everything went black."

"How do you feel now?"

"My hand hurts."

As I lifted my left hand, I saw the bandage.

"You received several stitches from a cut you must've received from the fall. You're lucky that was your only real injury, or was it? Does it hurt anywhere else?" Jesse asked.

"I have a little headache," I replied, rubbing my right temple.

"Do you have headaches often?"

By profession, Jesse Barros was a journalist. She was also my best friend. Jesse had the annoying habit of always being more of a journalist and less of a friend at times. I knew it was her training, but there were times I'd felt I was being interviewed for her next article. I had to carefully monitor every word I said when around her.

"Jesse, give it a rest already; you're not my doctor. Don't you think you should leave this to the professionals?" I asked her. "What time is it?"

"It's a quarter past two," Jesse said angrily.

4

"Oh, Jesse, we've got to go; Carina will be getting out of school soon."

As I tried to raise myself, the slight pain in my head rose from a low-pitched hum to a full scream. I immediately sank back in the bed. The pain was so intense I thought I was going to faint again; at least, this time, I was already lying down and couldn't hurt myself. The headaches were more frequent now. At first, they'd happened only every once in a while. Recently, it seemed they came at least two or three times a week. I'd blacked out only once before, and it had been a momentary flash.

"Just relax! The nurse went for the doctor. The kids will be fine; I've already taken care of that. Your housekeeper has agreed to pick them up," Jesse said with a hint of pride in her voice. "I didn't just sit here while you were out. I even called Sebastian's office to let him know what happened."

"Sebastian's not in Germany at the moment. What is she going to do with the children?" I pondered aloud.

"She said she'd stay with them until you came home," Jesse responded.

"We've got to get there right away. She wasn't hired to be a nanny. Carina will not be happy at all," I said to her, getting up more slowly.

As soon as I got to my feet, the doctor came in and asked me to lie down. I wasn't about to explain to another doctor what had been happening to me, especially with Jesse present. She wouldn't understand, and could have complicated things even further. I had to convince the doctor I was okay and get him to let me go home. How was I to do this without raising suspicion with Jesse?

"Listen, Doctor, what's your name?" I asked.

"I'm Dr. Heinrich," he replied.

"Dr. Heinrich, I really think I am fine. Maybe I tripped on something. It was just a clumsy accident," I began to explain.

"Well, Mrs. Schütler, that might be the case, but we should keep you for observation just in case," he interrupted. "You might feel fine now, but, until we know why you were unconscious, we should be cautious."

"Really, Doctor, I'm fine. I'll follow up with my family doctor. And, as you can see, I won't be alone. My friend here will be with me in case something else happens, but you needn't worry," I tried to assure him.

"Beatrice, let the doctor check you out," Jesse said, exasperated. "Didn't you just say to me to 'leave this to the professionals'?"

Normally, I would have adhered to the advice of any doctor.

However, two things were in play here that would not have served anyone. First, Jesse's eyes had lit up when the doctor entered the room, and her concern, although genuine, was also fueled by the doctor's good looks.

Did Jesse really think she could start something with this guy? She was only visiting from New York for a week.

The second was, if I stayed, it could've been awkward. Inevitably, I would have to explain the headaches had been happening for months now. I hadn't found the time to tell Jesse. That's why we were having lunch today. I wanted the opportunity to explain, in a private setting, and reassure her that I was fine. Although, it would have been the first of many lies I would tell her in the future. If she found out this way, she'd be furious. More importantly, I just wanted to go home.

"Jesse, you can exchange numbers with the doctor while I get dressed. Then we have to leave," I said.

"Beatrice!" she exclaimed, almost shamelessly.

Nonetheless, Jesse had done so while I got dressed. I knew my friend all too well, but, despite her perpetual flirtations, she was still my best friend.

Jesse would prove her loyalty time and time again over the next few months.

* * *

We had to take a taxi back to the house, since Jesse had ridden to the hospital in the ambulance with me. No doubt, there had been a gorgeous paramedic. The taxi ride gave me some time to formulate a different plan as I listened, or pretended to listen, anyway, to her ramblings about the cute doctor. I'd devised a plan to tell Jesse what had been happening to me before she arrived. That plan had to be changed, given the current events. I didn't think she noticed I was deep in thought. Jesse just went on and on about the doctor, and I nodded politely every now and again.

I couldn't get over the feeling that 'this', whatever it was, was happening too fast. Last week, I went to see my family doctor about the headaches. He'd drawn some blood as a starting point.

'Maybe it was a lack of rest', he'd said, 'or high blood pressure'. I tied to recall. I was starting to doubt the accuracy of my recollections.

He wanted to rule out all the minor possibilities before jumping into more serious things. I'd agreed with him about the course of action. All the while, I had a nagging feeling that 'this' was not minor in any way.

* * *

When we arrived, the door to the house opened, and my two little girls came out. "Mommy, Mommy!"

There were times when the word 'mommy' was a nuisance, like when my children had been fighting all day and I had to be the constant negotiator, or, perhaps on the thousandth and first question about a single subject. Then there were times when 'mommy' was called out in shear agony, and it hurt me to hear one of my children cry out in pain.

Yet, ever so often, 'mommy' was also music to my ears.

The *Hallelujah Chorus* sung by the Mormon Tabernacle Choir paled in comparison to the voices of my two children that day.

"Are you okay, Mommy?" Anna, the eldest, asked.

As I held onto my two girls that afternoon, something began to change within me. "I'm fine, sweetheart," I replied.

Then, suddenly, I was afraid. The weight of the day's events came crashing home in their presence. What if I wasn't fine? What if I…? I had to stop myself from asking that question. It was at that moment, holding the two of them in my arms, I'd been reminded of the promise I had made to each of them before they were born.

Their lives had to be different from mine.

* * *

"Listen, Jesse, I need to talk to you. And please don't repeat this to anyone. Not even Sebastian. Give me your word you will not say anything," I begged her.

"Okay. You have my word," she replied.

Jesse wasn't very good at hiding her anticipation. I saw her eyes glaze over as if she were about to receive a juicy tip of some sort.

"And don't jump to any conclusions, either. This is hard enough without your overactive imagination or journalist instincts speculating as to what it could be," I added.

"Beatrice, just tell me what's going on," she said.

"Today wasn't the first time I've had a black out. It has happened at least a couple of times before. This time was the first time I'd went out completely; before, they were only momentary. I saw my family doctor last week. They've run some tests on the blood he drew, and I get the results tomorrow. I need you here with me when I get the results."

Jesse just sat there. I was surprised, because it was rare to see her speechless. Her silence was a little unnerving. I was happy to see it didn't last too long.

"Oh, Beatrice, you must be terrified! Do you have any idea what it could be?" Jesse asked.

"Not yet! I'm so glad you are here. It's probably something minor. The doctor suggested it could be something simple, but he'd know more once the preliminary tests were completed."

There was no way I could tell her what I was really thinking. My thoughts were all a jumble, as it were. Trying to explain to her what I was thinking would have caused more alarm than I was prepared for, and, given her performance in the hospital, most likely more questions than I wanted to answer.

So many emotions, feelings, and thoughts had come over me in one day, not to mention my little fainting drama. By the time I went to bed, there was no problem sleeping. Jesse wasn't my only houseguest. Fatigue, previously a rare visitor in my life, had begun to move into my world to stay.

* * *

The next day, Jesse waited in the waiting room while I saw the doctor. I sat in his office, a bit nervous. I didn't know what to expect. Perhaps I'd even begun to prepare myself for the worst when he entered.

"How are you feeling today?" Dr. Koenig asked.

"I feel fine today. It's hard to imagine just yesterday I was in the hospital," I replied.

"Yes, I got the report from the hospital. I wanted to compare your blood work from the hospital to when you were last here. Your white blood cell count is even higher than it was on the first test. Beatrice, this, frankly, concerns me. When we see the count this high, it could mean many things. Some are serious and some are not. The most important thing one tends to think about is the body is fighting infection of some kind. There are other considerations to take into account, too. What can you tell me about your family medical history? Any major illnesses you might remember?" he asked.

Somehow, I knew it would come to this.

"Well, Dr. Koenig, both my parents died in a car accident. As far as I know, they were both healthy. I don't remember much about my grandparents, really. I do have some vague memories of stories being told about my grandmother dying young. I was a child when I heard this, and was not sure then what it meant. If memory serves, she died at seventy, and that's not young to me," I answered.

"Well, no, seventy is not all that young, but do you know what she died of?" he asked.

"No, I'm afraid I don't."

"Do you know if it was a long illness?"

"I'm sorry, Dr. Koenig, I don't know that, either."

"Did your grandparents live here in Krefeld? Or do you know who their doctor was?"

"Yes, they were from here, and I think they saw your father, if I'm not mistaken."

"Well, if that's the case, the records will be easy to find. What was your grandmother's married name and maiden name?"

"Well, her last name would have been the same as my grandfather's, Stiegel, and I'll have to call you with her maiden name. I don't remember it off hand."

"That's fine, Beatrice. In the meantime, I'd like to run some more tests. Unfortunately, it will require a day or two in the hospital. Now don't be alarmed; there are some things I'd like to rule out."

"What kind of test, Dr. Koenig?"

"I'd like to do some additional blood work and to have an MRI and a CAT scan of your head for precautionary measures, since you said all this began with headaches."

"Can those procedures be done as out-patient?"

"Yes, under normal circumstances. But there are some additional things I'd like to explore and, depending on the results from the MRI and CAT scan, there could be some delayed reactions. It would be best to observe you in the following thirty-six to forty-eight hours after."

"Whatever you think, Dr. Koenig. How soon would you like to do the test? I'll need to arrange a sitter for the girls."

"Beatrice, I'd like to do them today. Once you've got the children taken care of, give my secretary a call and we can get you into the hospital as soon as possible."

"Oh, Dr. Koenig, I can't do it today. I have a houseguest, and the girls will have to be prepared. No, I can't do it today. What's the urgency?"

"Beatrice, with the complaints of headaches and with the recent addition of your blackouts, I want to be aggressive, again, as a precautionary measure. The sooner we resolve the question as to the illness, the sooner we can begin treatment," he said.

"What do you mean begin treatment? What are you not telling me, Dr. Koenig?" I interrupted.

"I'm telling you not to get ahead of yourself, and I want to be cautious," he said sympathetically. "As I said before, it could be a number of things. But, with the combination of headaches and blackouts, it could be something very serious. With these tests, we can get an accurate diagnosis instead of an old man's speculation."

"Sure, I understand. I can't today, however. I'll arrange something with the girls and get back to you. My houseguest will be leaving soon, and then I'll be free. Would you mind if I had a moment alone?"

"No, not at all; take all the time you need."

I felt numb and weightless. For a moment, I was floating above myself, saying, 'this isn't happening to me; you are watching a bad TV program'.

The sound of the door closing snapped me out of my trance.

I couldn't let Jesse see me like this. If I'd walked out of his office looking half dazed, she'd have never let up. Jesse would leave in a few days, and I could resume the nightmare on my own. I'd said to her, just yesterday that I couldn't take bad news alone. I was wrong. I didn't want anyone to know.

As I entered the waiting room, Jesse sprang to her feet. There was a moment's hesitation before she came to me. "Well?" she asked.

"Everything's fine," I said.

"So, tell, what's the problem?" she asked again.

That was Jesse, straight to the point.

"He's still not one hundred percent sure, and I need more tests. But the doctor doesn't think it's serious," I lied.

The first lie was so innocent. Almost as if the words had significance, and then, just as quickly as they came out of my mouth, they didn't.

"Oh, thank God, I was really worried," she replied.

"There's no need to worry; I'll be fine in no time…" I lied again.

There was no mistaking the difference of the second lie from the first, however. Something moved inside me; a shift from one plane to another. I felt the loss of something I couldn't get back. Yet, I couldn't pinpoint the nature or type of change.

* * *

The first few days after my second visit with the doctor were hell. I kept going over and over his words: 'it could be something very serious'. What if I was seriously ill? How would I manage an illness, of any kind, serious or otherwise? Life in my house was challenging enough without something else getting in the way.

Jesse had been a great help, but I was anxious for her to leave. She had to leave before Sebastian came home, anyway. The two of them together would have been too much to deal with. Then there was the problem of finding time for the tests the doctor wanted me to have. How was I going to arrange this without raising suspicion? I didn't want to tell Sebastian right away. I told myself it wasn't worth the trouble of having both of us worried over nothing. My decision to wait to tell Sebastian wasn't a popular one with Jesse.

"What do you mean you're going to wait to tell him?" Jesse asked.

"Well, what if this is nothing to get excited about? There is no use worrying everyone. When we know what's wrong, then I'll tell him," I rationalized.

"I think you're making a big mistake not telling Sebastian. He deserves to know. And you shouldn't have to deal with this alone."

"I'm not dealing with it alone. I have you, right?"

"Of course, you have me. You'd do the same for me in a heartbeat; I know that. But not telling your husband is another story," she said. "Remember your vows, in sickness and in health, richer or poorer… He needs to know, Beatrice."

"And he will know, just as soon as the doctor figures out what's wrong with me. He

11

has enough on his plate without me adding to it," I explained.

"Beatrice, his burdens are yours, and vice versa. Don't you think he'd like to be there to help you through this? I think he would. You two are the best-suited people in the world. I'd love to have what you have: comfort, security, and, most of all, love. Besides, what if he was to find out you've kept this from him?"

A flash of anger rose in me so quickly I couldn't control the words I said to her next. "Don't betray me, Jesse. Need I remind you, you swore yourself to secrecy? You're the only one I've told, so, if Sebastian found out, it could mean the end of our friendship."

* * *

Jesse and I had been friends since our university days. Her initial college years were solely based on the attention she received from the boys. I saw her through every triumph and failure, and there were many. More than once, her little love forays ended badly, and I was there to help her get through the break up. I never had such moments with boys. I was too focused on my studies. However, Jesse was there, nonetheless, when I was distraught about grades or anything else. We'd relied on each other then, and there was no doubt in my mind she would rally around me again.

My words about her betrayal were harsh, but we'd overcome much worse in the past. If necessary, we would need a day or two to cool off, and all would be forgiven. However, before she left, I had to make things right. She'd have a much bigger part to play in the future.

"Jesse, I want to apologize for what I said the other day. I didn't mean it. I am just tired from the silly drama of the past few days. Not to mention Sebastian and I are having some problems," I said.

"Oh, really, trouble in paradise… Not you two," she said. "Despite whatever problems you two maybe having, this could be the thing that helps you resolve them, or at least get you back on the right path. In times like this, these things often help you see what's important." I knew there was a good reason why Jesse and I were still friends. She may be a shameless flirt, but she always had good advice. The words 'what's important' stung a little, too, but not because I thought Jesse was being cruel. I knew what was important to me. I was having doubts, for the first time in my marriage, if Sebastian knew what was important to him.

"What exactly is the problem?" Jesse continued.

"Oh, it's nothing catastrophic. I suppose it's just me. Well, I have mentioned to Sebastian how much time he works. I've even been a bit confrontational at times about it. It seems to me we don't spend as much time together as a family. I am sure he is aware of it, too, so my not-so-gentle reminders haven't helped," I said.

"That doesn't seem to be an insurmountable problem. I am sure you two can work it out. Is there something else?" Jesse asked. "You know you can tell me anything."

Obviously, the weak attempt I had just made at a plausible excuse was not working for Jesse. She would need something more substantive to chew on.

"Well, you're right; it's not that difficult, but the tension has spilled over into the bedroom. We haven't been intimate in a while now," I said.

As I said the words, I wasn't totally lying. It was true we hadn't been intimate in a while, but Sebastian's work schedule had nothing to do with it.

For some time now, I'd thought Jesse might have been a little jealous of Sebastian and me. I felt I had to say something to appeal to her sense of balance. I wanted her to know all was not paradise. The intimacy issue was meant as a token or a window for her to peek through and see what was happening in my little world, and it wasn't at all happy. Jesse and I hadn't had a chat like this in years; she just assumed all was well.

"I am sure things will get back to normal soon. I think every relationship goes through moments like that," Jesse said in her most reassuring voice.

"Listen, I don't want to complicate things any further by dumping more on him than is necessary. We need to resolve things on our own, not because of some outside influence or illness," I explained.

"Well, I still think you should tell him, but you know your husband better than me. Just tell me you won't let it go for too long."

"I won't. And, Jesse…Thanks for being here."

"You're welcome, you know that. Promise me you will come to New York City soon and we can have a real girls' night out."

* * *

The day Jesse left was one of the longest days of my life. I wanted her to leave, but, the moment she did, I felt alone. I tried to go about doing my normal routine, but found myself sitting at my kitchen table, staring into space with a million questions.

I had never been the type of person to plan for every unforeseen event that could go wrong, nor had I been the kind of person who asked 'what if' this or 'what if' that, but, as I sat staring into space, the 'what ifs' started to preoccupy me more than I would have liked. The void I was looking into suddenly narrowed. The possible future of promise and possibility had been replaced by doubt and fear.

Questions I should have been asking of my best friend, or maybe my husband, found no ears to fall upon. Instead, I was taking a 'wait and see' approach, which didn't allow me to confide in anyone; a conscience choice, but a lonely one, too. My biggest fear was that I was no longer sure of anything. Doubt was the best friend and husband of fear.

Moreover, if I was afraid or unsure, what would that do to those around me? I didn't want anyone to worry unnecessarily. So far, there was nothing to worry about, I tried to pretend. Sebastian had his work, and I didn't want to get in the way there. There would be plenty of time for him to worry if there was something seriously wrong with me.

Anna and Carina were just children; they shouldn't have such concerns at their age.

Jesse was my best friend, but she was overbearing at times, and that was really it.

Those were the people I was trying to keep from 'worrying' about my health.

* * *

The arrangements for the hospital stay were easier than I'd thought. Sabine, Sebastian's mother, called and suggested a visit. How could I refuse? The girls were set. The only remaining problem was Sebastian.

With him, I had a bit of luck as well; a trip came up at the last minute. Contrary to how I'd behaved in the past, I said nothing. Sebastian noticed this, too.

"Are you sure it's not a problem?" Sebastian asked.

"Really it's not a problem," I replied.

"What's happening here? You're usually not so agreeable when these last-minute trips come up," he commented further.

"Well, I have decided to take your mother up on her offer for some time alone. With the girls at your mother's and you on a trip, I thought I'd meet Jesse in Paris. She's covering something there, and she's been after me to have a girls' weekend. So, I thought why not," I said.

The mere mention of Jesse's name turned his thoughts way from my lack of concern about his trip. Jesse was not his favorite person in the world. Sebastian always referred to her as the Devil's daughter.

He didn't know Jesse like I knew her.

Not that it mattered, because there was no truth to this little white lie, and, again, this first lie to my husband was really as innocent as the first was to Jesse. There was no real harm to anyone. My true whereabouts were a benefit to the future of us all. Besides, I thought he'd be less interested in what I was doing if Jesse was involved, and I was right.

However, the nagging feeling of loss with the second lie to Jesse came back with equal force. Jesse was one person I could lie to and be easily forgiven. She would see it like I saw it: necessary. Sebastian, my husband, was different. I wasn't so sure he'd agree with my logic. However, arguing the point was too late.

* * *

The only thing left to do was to call the doctor and schedule the tests.

The hospital was the last place in the world I wanted to be. One of the main reasons I followed through with the doctors' orders was fear. Fear of being discovered and fear of causing harm to my daughters. I also had a general fear of hospitals.

When I was a child, it seemed as if my mother and I were in a hospital on a weekly basis visiting someone. My mother would drag me with her as if it were a fun outing of some sort. The most prominent memory of those visits was the smells.

I had no idea the smell of disinfectants, what I considered old and sick people, would have such a lasting effect. It consumed me as I entered the hospital doors as a child, and has lasted until this very day.

The tests went off without a hitch.

In fact, they went so well I was released after having only spent one night in the hospital. I was told to see my doctor on Monday, and I left. I walked away feeling as if the problem had been found and there was an easy solution. I had all of Saturday and most of Sunday alone, as proposed.

There was only one odd thing about the whole weekend.

When I arrived home, there was a message from Dr. Koenig. He asked me to make sure I followed up on Monday in his office. I thought it was very nice of him to call, personally, to confirm the instructions of the hospital. The fact that Dr. Koenig doesn't keep hours on Saturday should have registered something, but it didn't.

However, on Monday, I became alarmed when the doctor's nurse called to confirm the appointment, too. At first, I thought Dr. Koenig must have forgotten he called on Saturday. That's when it finally hit me. He had called on a *Saturday*.

My thoughts abruptly switched to one of my original questions: what was the urgency? I stopped preparing lunch for the girls, and stared out the window; more 'what ifs' started growing in my head by the minute. The housekeeper came into the house and snapped me out of my trance. I had to put on a brave face for her and the girls. There'd be plenty of time to sort this out on the drive from school to the doctor's office.

As I drove from home, the questions took over again. What if I was seriously ill? How would I manage? How would the girls manage? How would Sebastian take the news? Again, I was startled back into reality, this time by an irate driver who had been behind Anna and I.

"Are you okay, Mommy?" Anna asked.

"Yes, honey, I am fine," I replied.

"Well, if you don't hurry, we're going to be late," she said.

My practical little girl, she was. I had to laugh to myself for a moment.

With the girls settled into school, I could slowly make my way to the doctor's office.

* * *

"Beatrice, I need to ask you some very important questions. What do you remember about your grandmother? Is there any one thing you can recall about her physical appearance?" Dr. Koenig asked.

"Only that she had red hair. It was one of the things my mother commented on frequently, and not in a positive light!" I joked.

"I am sorry to have to be the one to tell you, but that was not your grandmother. The woman you knew as your grandmother was your grandfather's second wife. You would have never known your maternal grandmother, because she died long before you were born. She was the one who 'died young', as you said. I can see how it might have been confusing for you."

"But what does that have to do with me and what's happening now?"

"Well, medicine was a lot less advanced then. There were illnesses we had not yet identified, for example. People died without the benefit of what science can offer us today."

"Dr. Koenig, I appreciate the history of medicine lecture, but could you please tell me the results of my tests?"

"There's no easy way to say this. Beatrice, you have cancer. It's called Khan's lymphoma cancer. The reason I asked about your grandmother is because she may have died from it. Recently, science has discovered it sometimes skips a generation. It seems to fit your case, as you said your mother was healthy. Your daughters should be tested to verify whether or not they have the actual disease or carry a trait."

"Fine. Is there a cure?"

"I'm afraid there isn't"

"I see."

"Unfortunately, there's more. The cancer has metastasized to the brain and created several tumors. One of the tumors may be the cause of your fainting spells. We can give you some medication to help with the fainting and the dizziness. You have to understand, these measures are temporary. Surgery is possible, and might help on a more permanent basis. However, the risk is considerable. Best odds are a fifty-fifty chance. The other thing to consider is, even if the surgery is a success, there is no guarantee it will prolong your life. In fact, it could shorten it," Dr. Koenig said.

"Do you recommend the surgery?" I asked.

"I wouldn't venture an opinion. I think you should consult another doctor better experienced in such procedures. I've spoken to a colleague in Cologne about you. He said he'd be happy to review the findings and what options you have with you and your husband. There are some treatments we could explore. If you had been diagnosed earlier, there might have been some therapies available to give you more time."

"Did this doctor say how much time I might have?"

"He said in cases similar to yours, eight to twelve months without significant changes; with a successful surgery, maybe longer. You will deteriorate and eventually have to be hospitalized. I've also taken the liberty of contacting a psychiatrist who specializes in such cases, and not only for the patient, but the family, too."

"Thank you, Dr. Koenig; that's very kind of you."

"Would you like to have some time alone?"

"No, you must have a busy day, and so do I. Thank you again."

"If I can be of any further assistance, please do not hesitate to call me. I'll give you my home number. You can call day or night."

"Thank you, Dr. Koenig; I appreciate your candor. I'll be in touch."

"In the meantime, I've written some prescriptions at the suggestion of my colleague to help with the fainting. I'll need to know about any new symptoms you experience, and I'd like to see you every other week. You should see my colleague in Cologne as soon as possible. There will be serious decisions you and your family will have to make in a short time. May I ask you one additional question?" he asked.

"Yes, of course."

"This may be a bit premature, but do you have a living will? What I mean to ask: are there any specific instructions as to your care in the event you become incapacitated?"

"No, I don't. We've made arrangements for death, but not that."

"Well, unfortunately, I think you should consider doing so."

"Yes, thank you again, Dr. Koenig. I'll look into it."

"Are you sure you are okay to drive?"

"Yes, yes, I am fine. I'll be in touch."

As I left the doctor's office, I wondered who I was trying to lie to more: the doctor or myself. The diagnosis was a fact I couldn't lie about. I might have been able to lie about how I was feeling to the doctor, but there was no way I believed what I'd just said.

I wasn't fine at all.

In fact, I had already told the first of many lies to my best friend and my husband. Where would it end?

Chapter 2

Almost immediately, a trio of recurring dreams began.

The first dream was of Anna. She was preparing for a special day, maybe a graduation or something like it. She was frantic and having a hard time in her preparations. There was a certain amount of anxiety on my part, too. I wanted everything to be perfect for her, but it seemed the more I tried to help, the more distant I became. I would reach out to touch Anna, and her image would fade away. The dream never seemed to come to completion.

Initially, this dream was short, perhaps only a few seconds. Then, with each occurrence, more of the story would develop. It was weeks later before the dream in its entirety finally surfaced.

The second in the trio took place on the day my parents died. This dream wasn't as ethereal as the first. Here, the images were of the car accident itself, which I'd never witnessed. I could only assume the imagery came from the information I had read in the reports. Yet, they were as vivid as if I had been at the scene and, somehow, had taken part in the aftermath. The sounds and smells were all too real at times. I wished I'd never read those reports.

The last was by far the most pleasant of the three.

In this particular dream, I was always smiling. I was a little girl; I was happy. The sun was shining, and I had time to play as long as I wanted. Night never came. Also, in the dream, I had a playmate, someone I could share things with. We wore the same dresses and laughed for hours and hours.

On the mornings after I had that dream, I felt as if I could conquer the world.

My reality was nothing like my dream. I was an only child. The majority of my childhood seemed gray, sad, and sullen. Not all, but most.

The dreams had several effects. As they came and went, I wanted to classify them into categories; simple categories, such as good and bad. The good ones made me laugh and the bad made me want to cry, but even the bad ones became important.

However, life was not always that simple. Most dreams were based on memories, and memories served as a reminder of what life was like; what I might have learned; how I might change the future. Some memories were painful and others were the most precious things I could hold onto. All memories were permanent, however; indelible marks on a person's life.

The memories I recalled as I rambled around my house were a mix of good and bad, painful and precious, ugly and beautiful. Every room reminded me of what my life had been; with no hint of what it would be in the future.

The nursery was the first room to have been changed; Anna and Carina had their own rooms now. I'd only recently completed the change into guestroom. I wished it was still here now. The plans to remodel any further would have to wait, but I could still remember how it used to look and how it made me feel.

One of the happiest days of my life was when Anna was born. After seven hours of labor, the nurse placed this living, breathing small person in my arms. For the first few moments, I couldn't believe I had created something so beautiful.

We were both crying.

Anna was crying as her first act of life. I was crying because she was what I wanted most from life. I didn't think I could ever be that happy again. Then Carina was born. With my second daughter, everything doubled, including the happiness.

When my daughters were born, I made a promise to them and to myself: their lives would be different from that of my mother's or mine.

As I descended the stairs, I stopped and stared at the sofa.

My mother married an American soldier who had brought with him all the attitudes of privilege he thought were God-given rights. He was a man; therefore, he chose how they lived. My mother was a simple extension of the man. When I came along, I was an even lesser extension. I felt insignificant for a large part of my life under their shadows.

To my surprise, my father insisted I attend an American university. Initially, I wanted to believe he was softening as he got older, but there was no truth to it. My attending university in the US was an exercise in getting everything that was 'due' to him from the military.

What did my mother feel?

My mother always required my father's approval. Sometimes, it was asking for a simple compliment. "How was dinner, dear?" she'd ask.

A dinner she'd prepared to perfection on many nights. My father never took notice. Then, at other times, she was asking his permission, particularly when it came to spending his money. "The sofa is practically worn out, dear. I'd like to start looking for a new one, if that's okay," she'd asked.

In fact, every household purchase of more than €50 began in such a manner. As a first-hand witness to my mother's constant humiliation, I pitied her. I swore I'd never be in such a position, and I promised myself my children would not be raised in such an environment.

Had my mother made a similar promise to protect me? I also wondered if she had kept it. If her life had been half as miserable as I'd perceived it, how could she?

What I had witnessed as a child determined my life. I came to understand this only when I grew older. Perhaps such promises were made by all mothers when a child was born.

I also promised to protect my daughters in any way I could.

Mothers were supposed to do these things for their children, no?

There were two matters foremost on my mind when the doctor told me I was dying: Carina and Anna. For years, I'd given them the best a parent could give. I taught them many basics before they'd entered pre-school. They were the first to read in their classes. They were ahead of their classmates in many respects.

When Anna started talking, I saw the first fruit of the seeds I had planted. When she started kindergarten and the teacher told me she was much smarter than the others, I knew I had laid the foundation of a good life for her. So I made sure I repeated the things I had done before with Carina. They may have been born girls, but they would, in fact, have better lives than I.

They knew the alphabet before they were four, could read before they were five, and Anna started piano lessons at six. We spoke German in the house, but, a couple of days a week, I also spoke to them in English. I corrected them when they made simple mistakes most children made. Then, a day or two later, went over the importance of not making the same mistake twice. I was driven for their sakes.

Though my life as an adult hadn't been all that bad, I wanted my daughters to have an edge, and not just the things we as children were programmed to know. I didn't just want them to be better students. I wanted them to be better people.

There was nothing I wouldn't have done for them. I taught them, protected them, and loved them.

However, I would not be able to protect them for much longer. I wouldn't be able to keep my promise.

It must have been weeks after the diagnosis when I finally cried; I can't remember. However, I knew I hadn't cried for myself. I cried for my daughters. No one would ever love them as I did.

What would happen to them? Who would help Sebastian?

I began to dwell on those two questions daily. There was nothing that could be done for me, but I had to find a way to fulfill my obligation to my daughters.

Otherwise, everything I'd done to date would have been for nothing. The constant pushing and prodding, the weekly English lessons, the reading – all wasted. I couldn't imagine Sebastian doing any of those things with my – our – daughters. I had no choice, at this point; they had to become *our* daughters again. For so long, they'd been mine. Soon, I would not be able to call them *my* daughters, and maybe my daughters would be calling someone else 'mommy', somewhere in the future.

The questions, the laughter, the tears, the birthdays, the graduations, their weddings… I would miss these things, and there wasn't a thing I could do to prevent it.

You have cancer.

How could three little words change the course of a life so profoundly?

Then three different words raced through my mind: *it isn't fair.*

Yet, I also knew fairness had nothing to do with my particular diagnosis. Still, somewhere in the back of my mind, I wanted justice. Had I been given this particular sentence at a fair hearing, I might have been able to live with the diagnosis. I felt as if the sins of the mother were being revisited on me. A weak gene in the family tree, generations before me, and I was burdened with the heaviest price.

Then the real nightmare began.

Who would tell my daughters what they'd inherited? How could I prepare my children for the deaths of their unborn children? Was it naïve to think they would have boys and be spared the loss? Would modern medicine ever be able to cure this type of cancer? Unfortunately, they would have to be told. How? When? Who?

Would I have time to figure this out? I knew I couldn't answer all the questions in one day, but this question worried me more than any. Time became something else I was about to lose and, as I lost time, I lost life.

Surgery became out of the question. The odds were too risky. I'd have to take the chance that I could cope for as long as possible. I had to get answers to some of my questions.

To answer all of them might be impossible. At a minimum, I could get the major ones taken care of and deal with the remainder with some help later on.

Besides, there was no guarantee I had the time the doctor said. My first priority became clear: I had to fulfill my promise. I had to protect their futures. The doctor had asked me about a living will. I hadn't done anything so far, but now I began to consider it more and more.

My last will and testament would have to be the starting point. The money my parents had left me would give Anna and Carina some financial security; something good they'd inherit. Here, too, I could make sure some of my wishes were carried out. Yes, the will. Hopefully, in time, Anna and Carina would realize that I thought of them and acted accordingly.

I hoped they would come to the same understanding.

* * *

Standing at Anna's doorway, I thought about how they were unique.

Anna and Carina were as different as two sisters could be. Anna, my first born, was always more like Sebastian. From the time she could walk, she followed him around the house. She would sometimes wait by the door in the afternoons until he came home, and, during her first years, when Sebastian spent more time at home, she was always alongside him outdoors somewhere, emulating his every move.

Like me, Anna was also more practical. Once she understood something, she'd accept it and move on. Very few things bothered her for any length of time. Of course, she'd be upset about things, but she had always found a way of dealing with them; with a little help and a lot of questions. I was always there to answer the questions and to help her get through the struggle of acceptance. Who would do this in the future?

I loved Anna's strength, however. She settled for nothing. Another trait I'd like to think she got from me. Even though I knew Anna would rather chase after her father than spend time with me. I hadn't thought she'd ever stop following him around, but she had, when she was about five years old.

Sebastian was working more and more, and was often away from home on long trips. Anna seemed to take his absences as a matter of fact, almost as if she understood the nature of his work. I was surprised to see her priorities shift. She began to dedicate all of her free time to 'helping out' with Carina, and she was overly protective with Carina when other children were around.

While we were in town once, we stopped at a playground. I was talking to another mother when I heard Carina scream. Immediately, I looked in her direction and saw Anna face to face with a little boy. As I got up to see what the trouble was, I saw Anna punch the little boy in the stomach. I couldn't get there fast enough to prevent her from then shoving the boy to the ground. When I reached them, she was on top of him and pounding him with her fists.

"What are you doing?"

"Mommy, he pushed Carina and made her cry," she responded, out of breath.

For an instant, I couldn't have been more proud of her. Anna had come to the defense of her sister, and, in doing so, had pummeled a little boy almost twice her size. I was astonished.

The moment didn't last long, however. The boy's mother arrived and scolded Anna for attacking her kid. I gathered my daughters and hurried to our car. After I had Carina safely in the car seat, I asked Anna what had happened.

"Mommy, he wanted the swing Carina was riding. She said no, so he pushed her off, and Carina is littler than he is," she replied.

Again, I felt a flush of pride come over me, so much so that I forgot to correct her grammar.

Even though she had been justified in her actions, though, I had to say something about resorting to violence as the first remedy.

Anna listened intently, and said she understood and that she wouldn't fight again, unless it was necessary. I picked her up, held her in my arms, and told her how proud of her I was.

Since then, I've never doubted Anna's devotion to her sister.

My thoughts turned to Carina as I entered her room.

Carina has always been the more reserved of the two. She was much shyer than Anna. When she started kindergarten, her teacher asked me if there was something wrong with her. The teacher was concerned, because, for the first few weeks, Carina always played alone. I had to assure the teacher my daughter wasn't anti-social, just extremely shy.

From the time she was born, Carina was my girl. Anna was a daddy's girl. Carina was a *mamma's* girl; she hovered around me at home. Carina was the more emotional of the two of them. We had a puppy for only three days a few years back. When it died suddenly, Carina cried for almost a week every time she thought about the puppy. In three days, she'd become more than attached.

Carina was the more stubborn of them; a trait in common with her father. If she made up her mind as to how anything was supposed to be, it was hard to get her to change it. Not entirely difficult, but a challenge. We had many contests of wills in her early years, and, more often than not, I was the one to give in. I had only to think of my own childhood and I would capitulate, but it did make life a little hard at times.

For years, Carina only ate certain foods for breakfast, lunch, and dinner, until I had to practically force new things on her; muesli is still her favorite, and, sometimes, the process to bring about a change took weeks. She liked her clothes a certain way. I was surprised at how someone so young was so deeply in tune with her personal appearance. Her bed had to be properly made before she would move the covers and then crawl in. I know I probably shouldn't have indulged her as much, but I didn't care, I had the time then. Now, the routine has become so more familiar it just made life simpler to do it her way.

This would be Sebastian's biggest battle. He would have to undergo a reeducation of many sorts in order to understand how this household worked.

* * *

It was no surprise to me, really, that Sebastian was the last person I considered in terms of my diagnosis; obviously, the girls came first. My cards had been dealt. The only thing I could contemplate was how to play the cards and when.

Sebastian's hand would be dealt further down the road. He might even get help from the dealer with his particular hand, or receive better cards. Although I hadn't quite figured out exactly what I was to do with the girls, my husband wasn't as difficult to plan for.

The question was: how much should I tell him and when?

If I had told Sebastian the day I got the diagnosis, for instance, I was sure it wouldn't have been good for either of us. In reality, there was nothing anyone could do to change the course of the diagnosis. The end result certainly wasn't going to change.

For years I'd wanted Sebastian home. Now, all of a sudden, I had the perfect reason for him to stay home, yet I couldn't tell him. I was sure Sebastian would alter his priorities to accommodate my illness. However, I didn't want the alteration to come about under those circumstances. As I told Jesse, whatever we had to work through had to come from a desire within as opposed to a reaction from an outside influence. There was a more important reason for me to withhold the information of my illness from him.

Pity!

I pitied my mother, and I did not want anyone to pity me. I did not want to see the same look on Sebastian's face.

I wouldn't have been able to stand the look of pity from most people, much less from my husband. Pity alone would have been unbearable, but, if Sebastian had to give up the one thing that has defined him for so long, it would have been more than either of us could handle. I had my regrets about certain choices; I couldn't do that to him, too.

All I knew was my life was ending before the best part had begun. The best part of life for me would have been when my girls married. I was hoping to help them sort out all the things women needed to know; the things my mother wasn't able to help me with.

It wasn't as if my marriage had been the best.

Trouble had been brewing for a while. I'd mentioned to Sebastian, more than once, how little time he'd been spending with the girls, and, although his absence had given me all the time I needed to educate the two of them, something was lost on the family as a whole. The scales had been unbalanced for far too long. Sebastian and I had done our own things and never bothered to question the routine. When I did start to question it, I failed to understand the blame had been equal. I wanted to blame Sebastian.

Sebastian would have never deliberately done anything to harm anyone, much less the girls. I knew he loved them; I knew he had loved me once. He'd carry water across the Sahara to make us happy, one bucket at a time. I also knew he would provide for the girls.

He'd made sure we always had the best. He'd argued for and against the best schools and the safest cars for their sake. When Anna started crawling, he made the house child friendly, changing electric sockets, and moving solvents to higher places or out of the house completely. Time and time again, he had proved his devotion.

Money was never a problem for us. My parents left me plenty, but Sebastian insisted he provide from his income.

"It's my job to take care of this family, not your parents'," he said. "That money is for our girls' futures."

So, we spent his money first.

However, I knew I never had all of him. Even for a fraction of a second on the day we were married, I thought he was somewhere else.

As I sat in our bedroom, I was immediately drawn to the all the images of our life in the room.

One of my favorite photos of Sebastian was taken long before I met him. In the picture, he was standing in front of a hut, looking out at the ocean. I couldn't recall where he was. I did remember him saying that the place was where he'd felt most at home in his young life. This was during the time he had begun one of his first adventures into environmentalism. I'd never realized how lonely he looked in the picture before, but it has always perplexed me as to why he felt more at home there of all places. Not so much that I've ever asked. I've simply given him the thoughts I thought he was thinking. Like perhaps what his future would be like.

Sebastian kept a part of himself hidden from not only me, but everyone.

Why exactly, I wasn't sure. He remembered our birthdays, our wedding anniversary, and the other important dates most men forgot. Sebastian called every night when possible when he was away. He did the majority of the things a husband was supposed to do – when he could.

That was our trouble: 'when he could'. Perhaps it was my fault, too. I just didn't see Sebastian traveling as much as he did. He told me he'd practically seen the world before we were married, so I imagined he had gotten over the travel bug. I knew Sebastian was an environmentalist. I thought he'd be *my* environmentalist. I thought we'd start a recycling or reforestation project somewhere closer to home. Then, when I got pregnant, again, I thought he'd be home more often, but that wasn't the case. To his credit, Sebastian did turn down the odd trip here and there. However, as soon as Carina was big enough to walk, his life of travel resumed.

In traveling half the globe to protect the environment, my husband was fighting for what seemed to be defenseless. In hiding the truth of my illness now from Sebastian, I, too, was trying to protect the defenseless. There were only two real beneficiaries: Anna and

Carina.

Sebastian and I had loved one another once, but, lately, we'd interacted only as friends. It was no longer like the days when Sebastian would sneak off from work and we'd make love in the middle of the day. Now, our relationship was more like what I'd imagined a nun's relationship must be to God. The idea of the man was there, and sometimes his presence was even felt, but, often, there was just not enough to hold onto.

I'd wondered occasionally if Sebastian had ever really loved anyone before me. His parents, Sabine and Rainer, were divorced when he was a teenager. Since then, he had had issues with his father. If he ever truly loved anyone, it was Sabine. The reverence with which Sebastian spoke of her even made me a bit jealous, but that wasn't very difficult to do. His relationship with his brother, Dirk, had been strained since their parent's divorce, but, when we got married, Sebastian did something that drove them even further apart. Dirk wasn't Sebastian's first choice as best man. Ty Walker, Sebastian's best friend, declined the honor.

Ty had been in our lives from the beginning. He was there, in New York City where he was living, the day Sebastian and I met at an environmental conference. Sebastian was visiting Ty, at the time, while on a rare family holiday. It was easy to see their love for the environment had forged a strong bond between them. At one point during the day, I found myself competing for Sebastian's attention.

Sebastian and Ty's friendship changed shortly before we married. I found it a little strange, but I didn't pry until Ty declined to be best man. Sebastian denied anything had happened. He said Ty had become famous and forgotten his friends.

It was true that Ty had become somewhat famous. He was a novelist; a year or so after we met, he sold his first book. Sebastian said Ty had traded tents and trees for fame and fortune. I refused to believe that of Ty. Although I didn't know Ty as well as Sebastian, I never got the feeling he was the type to trade in a friend so easily.

Ty was a writer. He had been a writer when I met him and would be a writer, most likely, for as long as he could, and, with some writers, fame and fortune were part and parcel with the work.

Sebastian knew this, but couldn't be convinced otherwise.

In this, my husband and I had something in common at an early stage in our marriage. I, too, had been hard to convince about other women.

Even though I had no real reason to distrust my husband, I did have these little doubts from time to time. I guessed it was normal in most relationships, but it had been different for me.

My insecurities in the past had been many things; normal, they were not.

Jealousy has always been an element of our marriage and even before, at least on my part. When I started dating Sebastian, I lost a couple of girlfriends, because I thought they were after him. With one of them, there was an overwhelming amount of evidence. She'd sent him a letter, which he showed me. Needless to say, I was livid, but her little dalliance came first and made it harder for me to keep it all in perspective from that point on. It made me overly cautious and a great deal less likely to trust women in general when it came to Sebastian.

Then, when we got married, I stopped attending his work functions. I saw the way women looked at him, and I couldn't take it. I'd even seen men stare at him longer than I thought they should have. Every time I mentioned it to Sebastian, he would simply laugh it off. I thought he might have enjoyed the attention; who wouldn't, for that matter? Then he reminded me I was the only woman for him. Occasionally, I needed the reassurance, but it never seemed to last long enough.

My husband wasn't just attractive. That wouldn't have been enough for me. Sebastian had a great personality, too. His character made what some have called his 'classic good looks' all the more desirable. Sebastian listened and asked questions. His probing was not in any way trivial, but done with a true need to understand. I had never experienced anything like it from a man.

At times, I felt as if my confessions to him were somehow drawn out of me. I became almost defenseless in his presence. He had to do but one thing and my strongest arguments for or against anything would melt away: smile!

In many ways, it could have been said it was ordinary. If you'd seen Sebastian smile on the street, you might not have even taken notice. However, when you became familiar with the man, when you felt the intensity he displayed in every action or deed, when you were taken into his confidence, or when you felt the protection only he could give, that smile was a lethal weapon. It disarmed me, and even made me forgive and forget, and, although he might have been aware of the power in his smile, Sebastian was not the type of person to take advantage of it. When he wanted to win an argument, he wanted to do so because of the facts or what he felt, and he treated everyone else accordingly.

Sebastian's patience and genuine goodness pulled you in, and made you helpless and safe at the same time. He was never demanding, and always very considerate. For as long as I have known him, he has displayed a confidence like no other. It's as if he has always known what he wants and will not let anyone prevent him from reaching his goals. When you were around him, that confidence was inspiring and you worked or played harder because his confidence in you became your own.

I first witnessed this with the people who worked with him. They were all equally passionate about the work, I was sure, but some of the people in his office seemed captivated by him. I thought most would have risked their lives for him.

Many young girls would be hired only to have to be fired or quit because they were in love with the man and his passions. I knew this, because Sebastian had lit a fire under me once.

It took some time, but I finally accepted Sebastian had eyes for me alone. The hardest thing to do was watch Sebastian be himself and win the hearts of those around him so effortlessly. He could instill confidence where there was none. He could make you believe when there was no proof.

There was only one other time I let my jealousy overtake me. It was several years after we were married. Sebastian and some of his friends had planned to go to Turkey to protest something, and then they had planned to stay for several days longer after the demonstrations were over. I wasn't sure if his friends could be trusted.

When Sebastian announced this particular trip, I had to say I was suspicious. I trusted my husband, but I knew nothing about the people he was traveling with.

So, the week before he was to go, I made sure he'd never forget he had a wife.

We made love every night for a week. Each night, I'd done something different to heighten the passion of the night before: black negligees, wigs, themes, anything I could think of. If he was planning on having something with someone, he would have been too tired to do so after that week. I certainly was.

For some time, I'd kept my little jealousies under control. The thoughts still occurred from time to time, but they never lasted long.

* * *

Most of us have never realized that the choices we make today will inevitably lead us to our future; most of us never look that far ahead. Then I picked up the picture of Sebastian on the beach and asked myself something I'd never even considered in the past.

What was really on his mind that day?

If anyone had asked me a few months ago if I thought life was predetermined, I probably would have said no. I felt as if I had been given choices along the way: to listen to the advice of others or not, to participate in what life offered me or not, and to tell the truth or to deceive. The choice of one road over another could lead to very different lives.

I have often wondered where I would be if I had not married Sebastian.

All that I had today could have been just a dream.

Chapter 3

Deception became a new way of life for me.

As I attempted to keep those around me from worrying, I had to let something go. I wasn't sure yet what that was, so I chose to delay the truth. There was only one way to keep them all in the dark until I could get a handle on what was going on. I had to continue to lie. Lying to everyone was the only way I felt I had some control over what was happening to me. The doctor and I were the only ones who knew the whole truth about my illness, and I lied about almost everything concerning myself.

To Jesse, I lied about how I felt physically. To Sebastian, I lied about what I was doing during the day. I even lied to the girls from time to time. The justification of my lying to all of them was a way to protect them, and, the more I lied, the easier it became. The one thing I couldn't escape lying about to myself was my emotional state. No one was to ever see what I was truly feeling. I wanted to keep feelings out of the equation. If I wasn't lying about something, I was hiding something.

I hid the medication I was taking for the fainting spells that might possibly occur. The bathroom was out of the question. So, I had to find a place Sebastian would never look, and safe from the curious eyes of the housekeeper. My handbag was the only place I thought would serve both purposes. Then I had to buy something that locked. I couldn't risk the girls getting their hands on my handbag and the medication. The one thing I was most concerned about was if I hadn't taken the medication. What would happen if I fainted while driving the girls to school or while Sebastian was at home? I couldn't let that happen, so I took the medication without fail, but the fainting wasn't the only symptom I was experiencing.

Some days, I had to take long naps to have the energy to get through the evenings. Only Mary, our housekeeper, knew this. She'd even asked me once if I was pregnant. I laughed for a good half hour at this. Then I wished it had been something so simple, allowing me to let go with the shrug or a laugh.

Oddly enough, I knew that, as time marched on in all our lives, nothing in mine would ever be easy again. Visions of dark paths, hard choices, unanswered questions and more lies was what I saw ahead of me.

Nightmares in which I could wake from and have a different future, a different reality, were what I'd hoped for. I wished it had all been a nightmare, to be honest, but it wasn't. I scheduled the doctor's appointments for early mornings. I'd drop the girls at school, and then head to the doctor's office. Jesse was the only one who knew about my visits to the doctor, but she would never talk to Sebastian. She'd given me her word. Besides, Sebastian rarely spoke to her. He'd thought she was arrogant and pompous.

"I don't know what you see in her. I have trouble finding one redeeming quality in her," Sebastian had once said.

Jesse was the only one I could talk to about some of my new life. Even though she disagreed with me as to how I was handling all this. The truth of the matter was that I didn't really want her advice. I needed her to be a sounding board. She might have been arrogant and pompous to others, but she listened to me, and that was what I needed from her. What were girlfriends for? Now, she was more devoted to me more than ever. The little secret we'd shared was perfect for the curious mind of the journalist. Finally, I had become the 'story' she'd be a part of from the beginning. For me, she had become the confidant who would be able to answer certain questions later on.

There was one significant consequence, however. My deception made me suspicious of others, and I began to doubt the one person closest to me: Sebastian.

It wasn't only my deception that started this; the cancer was to blame, too. Or so I wanted to believe. However, before the diagnosis, I had not had such a trio of recurring dreams. There was no reason to think I wouldn't have been there for the important days in my daughters' lives, the death of my parents had been reasonably dealt with, and the happiest dream of the three had been a welcomed addition. Still, I struggled with what were my own insecurities versus what the cancer was doing to me.

As I regularly debated as to where the fault should fall, the dreams became a big part of my life during the day. I found myself thinking about them far too much. In fact, the questions of the nature of the dreams, why now, and what they meant, were as common as the question of what was for dinner. The more I tried to find answers, the more I came up with nothing.

Then it all changed.

Just as quickly as the dreams had started, one by one they began to resolve themselves. I had not been prepared for the resolutions, but how could I have prepared for any particular nightmare?

When the first dream of Anna was finally completed, I was devastated.

* * *

Anna was looking at herself in the bathroom mirror. From the look on her face, she wasn't happy about something.

"Did you find them, Anna?" Sebastian asked.

"Not yet! Did you ask Carina if she has seen them?"

"Yes, I did, but she hasn't seen them."

"Then they have to be in my room somewhere. I'll keep looking."

Anna then exited the bathroom and found Sebastian in her room. He was looking at her graduation dress.

"You are going to look so beautiful," he said.

"Thank you, Daddy, but you have to leave now. I am too nervous as it is. I'll find the earrings, I promise."

Later, Anna then picked up the dress, and a box fell to the floor. I tried to pick up the box for her, but I couldn't. My hand, not solid, could not grasp the box. Again and again, I tried, but with the same result: my hand passed right through the box.

I was a ghost hovering in the room and watching the scene from a distant plane.

I tried to speak, but couldn't. I tried to touch her face, but nothing – nothing. In the midst of the dream, my ghost self started to cry.

The stark and painful realization that I was dead was nothing compared to the next scene.

Suddenly, I was at the bottom of the stairs. I was standing next to Sebastian waiting for Anna. Sebastian had the video camera and was filming her as she came down. The feeling was very strange. I had always been the one to film such events for Sebastian.

As she came down, we both began to move back a step at a time. Sebastian was right; Anna did look beautiful, and, sparkling brightly on either side of her face, was the diamond earrings. Those earrings were the only thing of value my grandmother had given my mother. Again, the tears of a ghost started.

"This is for you," a voice said.

34

Whose voice had I heard?

I turned to see who was speaking, and a figure moved through me and started approaching my daughter. I was frantic. Why didn't Sebastian try to prevent what I felt was a threat to my daughter? I tried to grab this woman's shoulders, a woman I could see from behind, but was unable. I was as thin as the air, and couldn't prevent her from presenting my daughter with the flower she handed Anna.

My despair sank even further as Anna accepted the gift and moved forward to hug and kiss this woman.

* * *

I woke with the words 'don't you touch her' coming from my mouth. Sebastian, too, woke up and asked me if I was okay. I didn't answer him. I got up and quickly walked to Anna's bedroom to find her sleeping soundly and still a child.

My mind was in a muddle for days after that dream. The more I thought about this other woman, the angrier I became. Who was she, and why did she get to hug and kiss my daughter when I couldn't? She could do those things because I wouldn't be there.

That was when the first thought of Sebastian having an affair entered my mind.

Previously, the jealousy was a simple matter of how I'd felt when other women looked at my husband. This was very different; it was a feeling of anger I had never experienced before.

Who was this woman?

Could I be so easily replaced? Sebastian didn't know what was happening to me. How could he have found someone so quickly? Granted, Anna was older in the dream, but this woman was too familiar; the kind that took years to acquire.

I'd been able to rationalize many things since the diagnosis: lying, hiding my meds, and my own fears. However, this, I had a hard time with. This particular anger was more than irrational. Anna and Carina were my children. Mine! I was irreplaceable. I gave them life, fed them, bathed them, taught them, loved them…. and some stranger was about to move in on what was mine.

Who, and, more importantly, when?

If she'd only shown her face; if she'd made a simple turn so I could know who was to be my replacement. I became even angrier. The thought of another woman in my bed, with my children, hugging them and kissing them, almost consumed me.

For several nights afterwards, I was desperate to sleep. I wanted more of the dream to materialize; I needed to see her face. I wanted to see who was about to take what had been mine for years.

It was not to be.

The dream didn't come. Instead, I lay in bed for hours waiting for sleep to come. Nothing!

For several days, I was on edge with the thoughts of this woman, and it showed. I was short with Mary one morning. I had even snapped at Sebastian.

"What's wrong with you? You shouted at me this morning, and the other day at Mary; is there something you'd like to talk about?" Sebastian asked.

Are you having an affair?

Those were the words I had in my head, but of, course I didn't ask. I wasn't prepared for directness then.

"I'm fine. I'll apologize to Mary, but I haven't been sleeping well."

"I've noticed. You've never tossed and turned as much as you have in the past few nights. Bad dreams again?"

If he'd only known what a bad dream was. A bad dream was when you dreamed you woke up with no hair or walked into a room full of people, naked. This particular dream was the worst nightmare of my life.

To my knowledge, Sebastian and I had shared almost everything in life. Good or bad, we'd trusted each other enough that the other would understand. Now, that trust was rapidly evaporating on my part. Each time he left on a trip, I began to wonder if he was meeting other women. I'd even suspected his assistant, Dana. She was young and pretty, and managed his schedule like a pit bull guarding a bone. Dana understood Sebastian and his work. She didn't nag him about his children like I did. I wondered how many times Dana went on trips with him. I'd guessed all, but I wasn't sure.

When Sebastian left on this last trip, I'd found myself going through some of his things. I tried to tell myself it wasn't intentional. I was picking up after him. However, each item I put away questioned me, as if I'd been the one who had left them out and they were asking 'why'.

First, I went through his sock drawer. Perhaps it had been a strange place to start, but then I remember why I started there. The sock drawer was where my father had hidden money and things that were of value only to him. Sebastian was nothing like my father. Somehow, I thought it was a universal hiding place for men; nothing there but socks.

If I had been discovered looking through his things, I wasn't sure I could have even said what it was I was looking for. However, I didn't let that stop me.

Looking about our bedroom for the next place to search, I tripped on something I hadn't seen in years. Sebastian had left a pair of sandals at the foot of the bed.

Next, I went to our closet. On his side of the closet there were five shoe boxes. I was surprised, because I didn't think he owned five pairs of shoes. The shoes weren't in the boxes, of course; they were scattered about the house. A pair could be found at the front door, and another at the back. Not that he really wore shoes much to begin with. On our honeymoon, I bought him a pair of beautiful leather sandals, the very ones I'd tripped on, and they looked almost new. Barefoot was his preferred mode of dress, or undress, to be more accurate. In the summers, Sebastian's feet would be dirtier than both the girls' combined after having been outdoors most of the day.

The shoeboxes were neatly stacked one on top of the other. There were no identifying marks other than perhaps the label of the shoe company. I removed the boxes and sat on the floor in front of them, momentarily staring at them. My heart raced as I thought of the possibilities of what could be inside. I wasn't afraid. I was actually excited. I wanted to believe he was hiding something. This could be the 'something' I was looking for.
Then, I lifted the box on top, closed my eyes and removed the top. I thought this might ease the shock of an unpleasant surprise. When I opened them, I was almost embarrassed at what I had found. The first box contained a single framed picture of his family. They all looked so happy. Sebastian and his brother must have been teenagers when it was taken. The picture had to have been when his parents were still married. His mother wore a smile that beamed with pride; his father, stern but relaxed looking. I'd only met his father a few times before we were married, but he always looked sad. Even at our wedding, he seemed to strain at producing a smile.

My mind was immediately flooded with questions. Was this the last time Sebastian was happy with his family? Was this photo of a single moment when he felt whole? Why had he hidden it in the closet? Why was it not on display? Then I stopped there.

Obviously, the photo was a very important memory for him. Sebastian told me of the pain the separation of his parents had caused him, and here I was thinking the worst of him. I should have been embarrassed. Maybe this was the best way he could move on, and I was about to condemn him for some unknown reason. Something only I had felt and couldn't control. I had to get a hold of myself. If I wasn't careful, I'd drive myself crazy, and for no apparent reason.

I placed the box on top of the others and began to gather them up to put them back in the closet. *Is it really all that bad to see what is in the other boxes*, I wondered. I'd rather be embarrassed.

So, I sat again and removed the lid of the second box.

Inside, I found five things. There was a shoe, a barrette, a t-shirt from infancy, a piece of paper with one of Carina's first attempts at drawing, and a recent photograph. Sebastian had collected one particular item of significance to him during Carina's life. The first thought that went through my head was what meaning they could have had for him. With the exception of the photograph, none of the other items were really specific. They could have been from any child, but he kept them for some reason.

The third box was no different in terms of the childhood items, other than it was Anna's box. The significance of one item in particular was unmistakably clear. Sebastian saved a part of Anna's cast from when she'd broken her arm. He blamed himself for the accident that had caused the break. I tried to reassure him there was no way he could have controlled the fall any more than he could control the weather, but his guilt was not to be deterred. While Anna wore it, I could see the disappointment in himself on his face every time he looked at her. Several months after the cast had been removed, he finally accepted it was a simple accident, and, like Carina's box, an item for each of Anna's seven years.

The fourth box was mine. I knew it had to be. The weight of it was slightly more noticeable; more years, more items. We had been married, after all, for eleven years. However, what could Sebastian have hidden away that I hadn't already? Part of my self-imposed duties was to preserve as many family memories as possible. One reason, among others, I'd taped the events Sebastian was not able to attend.

Hesitation hovered around me. My breathing quickened and, for the first time, I looked around the room to see if someone might have been watching. Why did I hesitate? What was the reason? Like my memories, Sebastian's had been a mixture of good and bad.

Those that were bad, in his mind, weren't really. So, the things in my box had to be good, no? I didn't close my eyes again, but I removed the lid more slowly.

Positioned on top was something I didn't even have. Sebastian had saved the program from the conference where we met. I had sat in a chair, at a conference I didn't want to attend, and it changed my life.

Next, a preserved flower he'd picked on the trail where we'd been hiking the day he proposed to me. On the days I told Sebastian I was pregnant with our daughters, I'd written him notes. He had both and pictures of me and our daughters in the hospital on the actual days of birth.

From our wedding day, one of the handkerchiefs I'd had made. The first gift I'd ever given him, a leather bracelet. Then, there was a small photo album of our first environmental trip working together. Not surprisingly, dirt of some kind, who knows from where or when, and, lastly, an antique compass.

A tingling feeling near euphoria coursed through me as I studied each of the things Sebastian had so carefully preserved. Each of them alone would not have been identifiable to anyone other than Sebastian and me, but I was more than happy to have a small glimpse into what my husband had considered important to him.

However, the state of euphoria I'd been enjoying came to a full and stifled stop. One more box remained.

Looking at the last box, a sense of doubt was coming to a close. This time, there was no hesitation. I emphatically tore the last lid off the box with the determination of already knowing what was there. The evidence I was looking for uncovered.

Inside, I found a small bottle of sand, like a sample, a hotel receipt dated before the time we met, several leaves laminated and perfectly preserved, a CD, some sort of seed, and a feather.

Each item in the other boxes had been a single memory of the past years. Some of those things marked events, a trip, or perhaps something that happened that was very special to Sebastian only. Several of the items were unique to the three of us, his women, he once said; a part of Anna's cast, Carina's shoe or the lace handkerchief from our wedding day. The last box was the mystery. There was no way for me to identify who the person was. The things in the box were nondescript, and couldn't be associated to anyone I currently knew. I wasn't able to draw the smallest conclusion. They couldn't even be uniquely tied to Sebastian, other than they were his way of remembering this person.

Who was it?

The things weren't remotely feminine, but that was the assumption I'd made.

* * *

I needed some air. The search for some specter left me feeling a little lightheaded. Maybe a nice long walk would bring me back to my senses. However, I never made it out of the house; as I came down the stairs, the next piece of the puzzle was revealed.

Sebastian had left his backpack he used as a briefcase. So, I sat and went through it. There were files of current projects he was working on, files and maps of Chile, Peru, Brazil, and Argentina. I supposed they were the places he had been to recently or would soon be visiting. Sebastian was focused on saving the planet, but the majority of his work was in Central and South America. He'd recently been hired as a consultant for UNESCO, which would take him away even more, I thought. However, the only noticeable difference so far had been more reclusive hours in his study.

Sebastian's study was the next logical place to look.

I hadn't been in this room since the day we moved in. It looked much bigger than I'd remembered. When it was my father's study, the walls had been filled with mountains of books. Now, there was only one bookshelf and more maps.

The only times I'd ever been in the study before was when I was in trouble. My father would make me wait at the door until I was called in. Then I had to stand in front of his desk while he finished whatever it was he was working on. My father's desk was incredibly ornate, which made it appear more like a courtroom bench from which judgment was being handed down. He'd bark the word 'sit', and I would comply. At this point, he'd place his pen on the desk and begin his litany of questions.

The first thing to go after my parents died was that desk. I was paid a small fortune for it.

Sebastian had chosen a desk that was much more functional. His desk had a more scholarly quality to it and was definitely less intimidating. It beckoned to me to sit. From the vantage point of the desk, I could see every map in the room. Almost as a coincidence, there were neat piles of papers placed on the floor in front of each map.

40

This was how my husband worked. Each thing marked and placed together, either at arm's length or in plain sight. I got the feeling I had sat in command central of the world my husband was trying to save. Then another impression struck me. This room was much more orderly than any other in room in the house Sebastian had occupied. The neat appearance appealed to him. I'd only been in here a few minutes and it had appealed to me.

I also understood why he wanted no one near it.

It had been my idea for him to use it as his study. The idea was trying to give him a space in which to work from home, hoping he would be home more often. It hadn't quite worked out that way; one of my first attempts to manipulate my husband that failed. Had there been any logic to my searching? I was fully convinced he was hiding something, but what, I was not sure. While I was snooping at his desk, I found one drawer locked. My mind began to race with the possibilities. He was hiding something, after all. Why would he lock this drawer? We had no secretes, or, at least, I thought he had none from me.

The question then became where the key was. I looked in all the obvious places one might hide a key; like under an object on the desk. I looked underneath the other drawers to see if he'd taped it one of the bottoms. I'd seen that in a movie. I looked near the computer, under the computer. Then I'd imagined it would have to be somewhere close; he'd want easy access. So I sat in Sebastian's chair and searched again. I'd lifted everything; calendar, lamp, keyboard, monitor, books, pencil holder, and even the stapler. Still, there was no key.

By this time, I'd worked myself into an uncontrollable frenzy. I couldn't think straight. So, I left his study in a huff. I'd go back when I'd calmed down and could be more clear. As I left his office, the tea kettle began to sound off; I'd completely forgotten I'd started it. I made my tea and sat to think about this key thing even more. I wanted to know what was in that drawer as if my life depended on it.

The phantom woman was back in full force.

Then, of course, I began to think the worst. Maybe Sebastian wanted a divorce and the papers were in that drawer. Then I thought maybe there were pictures of her in there. There'd been none in the last shoe box. Why? If he saw her on a regular basis, there was no need for pictures.

I wondered to myself again; did Dana really go on those little trips of his? Was it somebody from his past? He'd seen many countries and probably known many women before me.

Could Sebastian have been having an affair because of our sex life? If that had been the case, I couldn't blame him there. We hadn't been intimate for some time, and even less so since my diagnosis. However, even before I was diagnosed, I'd been experiencing more pain than pleasure during sex. The doctor had said it was normal for this to happen at the early stage of my illness.

Pain was something I would have to live with; physical and mental. The physical, I could handle with the right medication. The mental would be a challenge. I had already started to experience mental lapses in my judgment. Was this part of my illness, or was it me being covertly suspicious? Forgetting my keys was a lapse in memory. What was my excuse for lapses in judgment?

Forgetting my keys; forgetting my keys; well, of course! Why hadn't I thought of this earlier? If the key wasn't here, it had to be on his key ring. Yes, it had to be there. On his key ring, it would be the most accessible to him at all times. He'd know where it was at all times, too. Now that I had solved the mystery of where it was, how would I go about getting it? Furthermore, was I prepared for what I might find? Just as I had finished that thought, the phone rang.

"How are you feeling today?" Jesse asked.

"Jesse, please don't start calling here every day and asking 'how are you'. I have enough to worry about without you calling daily for a health check."

"My God, it's only been a month or two since I found you comatose in your living room. You scared me to death, you know. What's got you in a foul mood today?"

"Oh, nothing probably, but let me ask you a question. I was in Sebastian's study, and I found a locked drawer. What do you suppose it means?"

"Well, it means, whatever is in there he doesn't want anyone to see," Jesse said. "And that doesn't necessarily include or exclude you."

"Exactly! He is hiding something, then. I knew it. What do you think it could be?"

"Bea, it's probably porn. I wouldn't get myself worked up if I were you."

"Too late!"

"Listen to me. A few months back, I had a problem with my laptop. I was trying to finish an article and needed to look up something; mine was not handy, but the current boyfriend's was. His Internet connection was already up and running, so I did what I needed to do, then snooped a little. I knew it was wrong, but what the hell, I'm a journalist. Anyway, I found files on his laptop that were password protected. Now, this guy wasn't working for the government or some clandestine agency. So, what was the need for protected files? When I asked him why, he gave me the password and said 'see for yourself'. Of course, I looked. The files were porn movies. So then I asked him why he needed them, and he said 'you are not always around when I'm in the mood, and for the times when you aren't in the mood'," Jesse said.

"But you were curious, right?"

"Sure, but you and Sebastian are different. I am sure there is a very good reason that drawer is locked. If I were you, I'd let it go. Everyone has something they keep to themselves. I think you of all people should understand that."

What I didn't bother to ask was what she was really referring to: my past before Sebastian, or not telling him I was ill. I hadn't even been honest with Jesse about what the diagnosis really meant. If she'd known, she'd have been here every day. I would tell her eventually; I just needed more time to process myself. I guess I was using the same excuse for not having told Sebastian, too.

"I was calling to see if you wanted to join me for a drink next month. You can drink, can't you?" Jesse asked.

"Yes, I can drink. What do you mean join you for a drink? Are you coming to Krefeld?"

"Not to Krefeld, but to Cologne. I have to attend some conference there, and I thought we'd have a girls' night one night while I was there. It's not often I get an all-expenses-paid trip out of the country."

"Of course I'll meet you in Cologne. I'll need a night by then, too, I am sure."

"Why do you say that? Something going on?"

"I've decided to tell Sebastian what's been happening."

"Bea, I am glad you've come to your senses. He needs to know. Who knows, this could be great for your marriage."

Death was not good for a marriage. However, I couldn't let on just yet.

"You're right; it could be," I said to agree with her.

If I hadn't, she might have pressed me as to why I hadn't, and that would be another mess to have to clean up.

"Then it's a date. I'll call you when I've got the tickets. Now, I have to get back work.

I've got a deadline to meet," Jesse said.

"Before you hang up, should I look?"

"No, I don't think you should; not without his permission. Ask him and let him tell you what's in the drawer. I think Sebastian will tell you. But you pay for drinks if it is, in fact, porn."

Not without his permission. I wasn't even really supposed to be in his study. How could I ask for permission? Once again, I hadn't given Jesse all the relevant information. So, how could I have expected her to understand what I was really going through? If she hadn't completely understood, how could her advice be of any use? I knew I was rationalizing, but it didn't matter. My mind had been made up before she called. Maybe I was hoping she would have said something to have changed it. I think, in all honesty, I was hoping she would have agreed with me. Maybe I would have felt less guilty then. I still had the opportunity to take her advice, and then I wouldn't have to feel the guilt at all. However, the anxiety was too much to bear. I had to see what was there, regardless of the consequences.

How would I get the key from his key ring? It had to be there. I'd looked everywhere else.

Sebastian would be back in a day or two. I didn't want to wait until then. He was in Berlin, or was it Hamburg? I couldn't even remember where this last trip had taken him. I could call him and ask.

"Sebastian, where are you?"

"I'm in Hamburg. Is something wrong?"

"No, I'd forgotten, is all. When are you coming home?"

"Well, I had planned on talking to you when I got back. I guess now is as good a time as any. Bea, I have to go to Argentina later this week. I'll be home tomorrow, and then out again the next day," Sebastian announced.

Panic struck me hard.

All I of could think about was getting that damned key. The past few days had been a torment. I didn't think I could handle much more without the pressure it was causing me to go unnoticed. I had to plan something. I'd only have one day to get the key and make a copy. How was I going to do it? I was so engrossed in my dilemma that something much more important had slipped my mind.

Anna's birthday was at the end of the week. Sebastian had promised he would be there. I was used to his surprise trips coming up. The girls had only just begun to adjust to his more frequent disappearances. They'd be disappointed, but they understood. Anna did, anyway; I wasn't sure it made much difference to Carina.

However, to neglect Anna's birthday again was asking too much. This would make the second year in a row. Last year, he left the night before the party without saying anything to her. Anna was sleeping and Sebastian didn't want to wake her was his excuse then. She had fun at the party, but she was not her usual jubilant self. When Sebastian came back, she didn't speak to him for a few days. Finally, Anna came around, but not without expressing how angry she had been. I was so proud of her.

"Bea, are you there?"

"I'm here!"

"Don't be mad; this has come up unexpectedly."

"I'm not mad. I'm well beyond that. It's not me you should be worried about. Have you forgotten what happened last year when you missed Anna's birthday?"

"Please, don't do that. I feel guilty enough as it is. But this can't be helped," Sebastian stammered in response.

"I know!"

When I hung up the phone, the feeling of panic increased. Time was not working with me, and, even though I didn't ask how long he'd be away, I knew a trip to South America would not be a short one. If I didn't get a copy of that key, I'd be in a bigger mess than I already was. What was I to do? I'd have to figure it out later. I needed to go back to his study and make sure everything was in its proper place.

* * *

The next day, I was only half aware of anything I'd done. By the time Sebastian arrived, I had worked myself into another half-crazed frenzy, and, in that state, an argument ensued.

"You said you'd be here the remainder of the week," I said, trying to keep my voice low so neither of the girls could hear us.

"Bea, I couldn't help it. This trip could provide us with some concrete research we need," Sebastian replied.

"Sebastian, our daughters need some quality time. Anna's birthday is this week, and you said you wouldn't miss it," I reminded him.

Sebastian didn't respond; he just picked up his suitcase and went upstairs to our bedroom. As he exited the kitchen, he dropped his keys into a bowl.

Now was the time to act.

However, I couldn't take all his keys. I didn't know which key I was looking for, and what if he came downstairs while I was out trying to have a copy made?

I started pacing again.

In reality, there would not have been enough time to do anything.

The situation was hopeless. We were also both mad, so the night was going to be a long one.

* * *

While preparing for bed, the idea came as to how I could get the keys. I could ask him to trade cars. If he took my car to be serviced, I'd have his keys and he'd have mine. This was the best I could do on short notice. The only problem was the car didn't need to be serviced. However, I could easily call the mechanic in the morning and ask him to take a look at it. The following morning, I got up early to try to sneak into Sebastian's office before he left. Since I didn't know which key I needed to copy, I thought I had better find out. I started the coffee in case he stirred while I was in his office. So far, I heard nothing. I took the keys from the bowl and proceeded to his study. I found myself tiptoeing down the hallway when it wasn't necessary.

As I grabbed the handle of the door, I froze; an alarm sound from upstairs. I wasn't sure if it was ours or the girls'. They were all the same. Either way, my little adventure would have to wait. Again, I tiptoed back into the kitchen and started to make breakfast. Not too much longer, I heard footsteps coming down the stairs. It was Sebastian and the girls. It must have been the girls' alarm, and they went to our room.

"Good morning, Mommy!" Carina said.

"Good morning, baby; sleep well?" I asked in response.

"Yes, thank you!" she replied.

Anna was silent. She was usually the more chipper of the two girls. Her silence was obvious. Sebastian must have already told her he was leaving again.

* * *

"I'm sorry *mein Schätzchen*; please don't be angry with me. Daddy will make it up to you when I get back, okay," Sebastian said.

"Okay," Anna said, without any enthusiasm.

"I tell you what, how about I drop you off at school this morning."

"Really?"

"Really!"

This was my break. If Sebastian drove them to school, I had to persuade him to take my car. There wasn't much choice, really; the car seat for Carina was in my car. If we traded cars, I could get his keys. I'd have plenty of time to figure out which key. I had to try.

"Sebastian, you'll have to take my car into town or put the car seat for Carina into yours."

"Do we have time for that?"

"Not really; why don't you just take my car? Then you could take it to the mechanic as well."

"Fine, but how do I get back when I return?"

"Well, I can leave your car at your office or pick you up when you get back; whichever is easier."

Problem almost solved, I thought.

* * *

One more wrinkle did arise before they left. Sebastian was incessant about the trading of keys for some reason. For a brief moment, I thought he might have suspected something, but how could he? It wasn't suspicion, he was protecting himself. His incessancy made me all the more daring.

"Did you switch the car keys, Bea?"

"Why don't you just take mine?"

"Because the office keys are on mine, and I need to go to the office before I head to the airport."

"Okay, I will."

However, I didn't do that. I still gave him my set of keys. I had an office key, too. I simply changed key rings. I thought, *he'll never notice.* Then I called the mechanic.

* * *

I was amazed at how such a small act of defiance made me feel. A spark of energy raced through me for hours, almost innocent in the initial stages, but it grew into something much more potent. The feeling was similar to helping an old lady across the street or giving up your seat to a pregnant woman; my body went warm and fuzzy. In addition, a small sense of accomplishment reinforced the feeling, and, upon completion, the charge was invigorating. Since the bad news, my energy levels had been depleted. All of a sudden, the battery had been recharged. Had it been necessary, I could have run a race, and probably won even. I liked the feeling; it was a very powerful drug.

How long could I go on with such a charge? Could I manage to recreate it? How? How could I do it again?

What would be the consequences if I continued to manufacture such incidents? Initially, I was also ashamed of the receiving such a charge. It didn't last long, however. The bad girl I had in me smiled. She was happy I had not forgotten her. In return, she found a source of energy I'd never experienced before, and she remained with me for the day. The giddiness made my daily chores almost fun. The day was spent in a wonderful and strange delirium, a kind or reunion of old friends. She reminded me of all the happy memories I had as a child, and hid the bad. Images of easy and light days flooded my mind. Days long gone, days I'd like to have again.

Plus, out of nowhere, I thought I'd heard a voice. The voice sounded so real, so warm and familiar.

"You can do it again," it seemed to whisper.

However, I knew I couldn't.

"Don't deny yourself. Days like this may be numbered. Good days will not come; you will have to make them. Little tricks like these are harmless. No one will get hurt. And, for each trick, think of the energy you will create for us. We could have many days like today.

Think of the fun we could have," the voice tried to convince me.

This time, I actually looked about to see who was speaking. Then I decided I was just being silly. I was talking to myself. I was alone; had been alone all day.

* * *

Days later, I had hours to snoop further. I thought I'd rush to Sebastian's study; instead, I wavered. I was acting as if my husband had committed a crime and I was planning to find the information to turn him in. Sebastian had never lied to me, and, until recently, I had never lied to him. However, three words had changed all that: 'you have cancer'.

Maybe I was starting to feel guilty, after all. Maybe I wasn't prepared to cross this particular line. One thing was for sure: once I did, there was no way back to this moment. Whatever I found, I could never let on that I knew anything. If Sebastian had ever suspected I'd betrayed him, I'd never be forgiven. Our marriage couldn't survive this, too.

I still hadn't told him I was ill. If I was going to do this, I had to be sure I could deal with the consequences. Lately, the decisions I had made had little consequence to my family. However, this would be such a breach of trust that it could do more damage than good. Plus, how would I explain myself? Was the satisfaction of my anxiousness more important than my marriage?

It didn't take me long to come to a final decision. Life as I'd known it had taken a turn for the worst. I wanted to live longer and I couldn't, and the thought of being so easily replaced by some stranger was more than I could handle.

More importantly, I didn't want any more surprises. My diagnosis would soon be enough for the both of us to deal with.

I found myself asking some of my previous questions as I walked to his office.

Could Jesse be right? Or I was using her rational of a way to save our marriage as a reason to snoop? If I found something derogatory, could I use it to save us?

However, if I believed Jesse to be right, did I have to adopt her philosophy, too? Was telling Sebastian the right thing to do? Were the two mutually exclusive?

Could I admit she might be right and not be inquisitive?

A small part of me knew there was no easy way of answering the last question. In the real world, the answer should have been 'the marriage was more important'; not only the

49

marriage, but basic respect for my husband. However, something in me had changed. The rules that should have applied to my marriage had changed for me. They could have changed for Sebastian, too, had he known what I knew. Armed with the complete knowledge of how our lives were about to change, I decided to think for both of us. I didn't allow myself to dwell on right and wrong too long. Everyone was better off with my judgment alone, as far as I was concerned. In time, we'd all share in the bad news, but, for now, I had to bear the burden alone.

With my hand poised on the drawer handle, I took a deep breath and opened it.

Inside, I found a metal box that looked as if it could survive a bombing. As I sat the box on his desk, I noticed it was locked. Fortunately, the key was still in the lock. Inside this box were all the important documents of lives: life insurance policies, wills, birth certificates, passports, car titles, deeds to the house and the apartment, and an inventory of both.

I sat the box aside and continued my search.

Next, I found six leather-bound journals. On the first page of each journal, Sebastian had written where he was, country and city, and the beginning and ending dates. He'd told me about Costa Rica and Panama, and how this trip had been the beginning of his career. I skimmed the pages of the first journal, not really paying attention. Most of what Sebastian had written was inconsequential to my search: plants, trees, animals, and soil sample readings… Training for future studies, I assumed.

The principal thing that made me continue was his penmanship. I'd never seen much of Sebastian's handwriting. He typed everything. Sebastian said his handwriting was horrible. What I found was beautiful block letters, with an almost child-like quality and perfectly written. In fact, it was so neat and orderly, I was mesmerized. It must have taken him hours to complete one day's entries. He'd certainly had the time then.

What made me press on was something very different. Sebastian began to talk about how he felt during this time.

To see the sunrise in Panama was like nothing I'd experienced before. The sun, on its gradual ascent, splintered through the trees… Light fractured and re-fractured by raindrops on the leaves; thousands of tiny beams without end, bursting into rainbows, searching for something unknown… until they *reached the top of the tree line, and then united to form the orange and yellow globe of daylight; silent, yet violently forcing itself on the day...*

Sebastian was experiencing the beauty of nature for the first time, and he was clearly moved.

Had I stopped there, I would have had a better and unique understanding of Sebastian. Instead, his words compelled me forward. I wanted to know more of his feelings. In his journals, Sebastian wrote about a time in his life I'd rarely heard him talk about, and it was intoxicating.

Had I stopped there, I would not have found the cumbersome path to redemption.

* * *

Over the course of several days, while the girls were in school and Sebastian out of the country, I finished all six journals.

Chapter 4

A strange thing happened as I was reading Sebastian's journals. My mood improved and I was less anxious. In fact, I didn't dream of the phantom woman at all. Instead, the third dream in the trio began to happen more frequently.

The playmate I 'played' with in the dream kept me from brooding. As I thought of her throughout the day, I was amazed at how my energy level would increase. Sometimes, I was almost giddy when it came to my daily routine. Then I began to daydream about her more and more, and got lost in another world. Hours disappeared while with my friend.

Many of the games we played in the dreams had been games of my childhood, card and board games alike. I'd taken part in some of the very same games with Anna and Carina recently. I didn't find it remarkable that my playmate's favorite game had once been mine: chess. I was also trying to teach the basics to Anna.

Then she completely took over my thoughts while I was daydreaming. Her influence had been subtle, but powerful; gentle whispers echoed through the hours of sleep and, when I was awake, guiding, probing, suggesting, and taunting me.

"We have work to do," she whispered.

"What work do we have to do?"

I got no response, but, less than an hour later, she was back.

"The game has already started… We need to catch up!" she said, whispering and fretful.

"What are you talking about?"

Yet, again, there was no response.

Whatever it was my playmate was trying to get me to do would have to wait. I had no time for games. I was late for the doctor's office.

* * *

"Forgive my lateness, Dr. Koenig," I said.

"Not at all. Beatrice, I would like to know why you've chosen to wait so long to tell your husband," Dr. Koenig said.

"How do you know I haven't told Sebastian?"

"Well, it would be normal for a spouse to call or visit me once they'd been made aware of the diagnosis. But Sebastian hasn't called. And you haven't asked me to speak to him. I just assumed you haven't told him. Am I correct?"

"You are. But I didn't come here to talk about my husband today. I need to know the absolute worst. What will happen to me if I don't seek treatment?"

"Beatrice, as your physician, I cannot advise you to forgo treatment."

"Your opinion has been noted; now, could you please tell me what will happen?"

"Well, as the cancer spreads, and more of the frontal lobe is damaged," he started. However, I was distracted.

Don't listen to him.

"…Patients often experience certain behavioral changes: risk taking increases; they might become impulsive and quick to anger…"

You aren't quick to anger, and what risks could you have? You are the one dying.

"…Some are fixated on a single idea or action… Hallucinations are not uncommon; auditory and olfactory…"

I am not a hallucination!

"Beatrice, I am concerned your silence is a symptom as opposed to simple denial," he said.

"Well, I haven't been experiencing any such symptoms. When and if I do, I'll let you know. I am sorry, but I need to go. I have to pick up the girls."

I couldn't get out of the doctor's office quick enough. It was hard to remember all the things he'd said, but I did hear the words 'living will' again.

As I sat in my car, I knew Dr. Koenig was right. I had to do something about a will. Sebastian and I had one will. We'd prepared for what might happen in the event of his untimely death as a precaution. He traveled to remote place and was exposed to far more dangerous activities than I. Now, I would have to prepare for my premature death.

Maybe Dr. Koenig was right about something else. Perhaps I was in denial. I'd just lied to the one man who could make sense of what the illness was going to do to me.

* * *

Betrayal was added to the list of my transgressions; I betrayed my husband's trust. My actions were clearly wrong. The very vows that were promised to keep us together, I'd broken. I had been misled by fear, jealousy and a dream.

In all honesty, love motivated me to continue reading Sebastian's journals. Love for the man standing alone on a deserted beach in my favorite picture; the ocean represented the world, and all that he had to face. Standing there, smoking, before he started the daunting task of wading through the minutia and the great. Love for the man who had written such beautiful words.

When I finished, I had much more than a simple understanding. For instance, I knew Sebastian's parents had divorced when he was a teenager. What I had not known was how deeply it had affected him. 'Ripped apart' were the words he used. The family Sebastian had known was no more. His father moved out, and his brother chose to live with their father; a choice Sebastian found hard to forgive.

Abandoned by his father and brother, Sebastian reacted with rebellion. He didn't elaborate, just that, he alone, was held accountable for an incident committed by himself and several of his friends. Sebastian never implicated any of them, and, as a result, he was sent to Central America for what he called a childish prank; thousands of miles away from home and the friends who had never spoken on his behalf.

He wrote:

I am more than alone, I've been banished.

As my mind tried to take in the words, my heart plunged into a melancholy pit. With less than ten words, Sebastian had moved me more than anyone had in years; words that should have never seen the light of day, much less my prying eyes.

Momentarily, I was ashamed at how easily I had presumed his guilt, and, having not found any on Sebastian's part, my own began to grow. I sensed the beginning of a constant fight between what was real and imagined, and my own fears and unfounded jealousies. I should have stopped and explored what I was feeling; let the darkness of the pit shape and mold my own heartache into something new, or perhaps let the growing guilt have some sunlight.

Still, I continued.

54

I learned Sebastian had been in love.

Sebastian had not written the words, but I could read it and almost witness the transformation. First, his writing style changed. He exchanged the childlike block letters for cursive; a clear signal to me of how the teenager was becoming the man. Second, the tone changed. He was more reflective in his entries. Sebastian wrote about the 'beauty' in the conversations he was having.

Who had he been talking to and what had they been talking about?

While learning Spanish in Costa Rica, Sebastian managed to make a friend. Soon after, they worked, played and traveled together, sharing dreams, ideas, and personal disappointments along the way. Sebastian had met someone as equally damaged as he was; he found a friend he could confide in:

I'm not alone anymore. I've found a special friend; someone who thinks and has been hurt like me. In a matter of days, we have developed such a complete level of trust, as if we've known each other for a lifetime already. I can say anything and not be judged for what I feel, but accepted because we have felt similar things.

Sebastian had found beauty in nature and a beautiful friendship.

Then the light of day violently crashed through my haze of ignorance.

I had been searching for a phantom… a faceless woman who didn't exist. The fear and jealousy of being replaced had clouded my ability to connect the dots. What I should have been looking for was someone who shared Sebastian's passion.

My husband had been in love with this friend.

Sebastian never wrote the name of his friend in his journals.

Once again, I should have stopped reading and given myself a moment to feel something, anything, but I didn't.

The environment had brought them together, but much more bound them together.

I have to protect my friend. We have to protect each other.

For several months, they were inseparable. Sebastian then expressed how he wanted to do things for his friend he'd never wanted to do before.

My anger had already been simmering, but, when I read that last entry, the pot boiled over. I threw the journal on Sebastian's desk and left his office. I was walking down the hallway when my playmate whispered, "Go back"

Confusion grabbed hold of my feet and halted my steps.

Then again: "Go back"

Normally, I wasn't one so easily swayed, but I needed to finish Sebastian's journals as a matter of fact. I couldn't go back to the time before I'd started the journals, so I had to go back to his study. There was no sense in stopping. It didn't matter if I'd read some of Sebastian's journals or all them; partial or total, betrayal was still wrong.

As I sat, I heard, "Finish what you've started."

Angry, confused and a bit afraid, I did. If I'd stopped earlier, and allowed myself to feel more for the words he'd written, my anger wouldn't have boiled over.

I refused to read any more of how Sebastian wanted to 'protect' his friend, so I picked up the last of the six journals.

GONE

The single word leapt from the first page, and my heart sank even further.

Glued onto the opposite page of the cover of the last journal was a photo of Sebastian's shadow. A machete was visibly producing another shadow of itself in the picture; nothing or no one else there with him that day on the beach.

Before I turned the next page, I knew Sebastian's friend had also abandoned him. It wasn't difficult to see the overwhelming pain he was suffering. The writing also demonstrated this. He returned to the block letters, although they were no longer childlike impressions, but that of a young man filled with sadness. From the depressions on the page, he must have traced the four letters a thousand times. The ink bled through to the next page, and I could see a distinct shadow of the same word. Sebastian had even written around the shadow on the following page as he tried to explain the sudden departure.

He started and stopped many times, and then marked through the words. Finally, he stated 'family obligations' had called his friend home. Sebastian also wrote that he understood. However, he felt something completely different; the frustration and disappointment were reflected in his writing once again. He no longer wrote about how he felt towards anyone. Instead, the words became cold and precise, and only involved what he called his 'work'.

Cataloging plants and animals counter balanced Sebastian's negative feelings to the world of people. Plants and animals didn't usually disappoint; people often did. Sebastian's obsession with protecting the environment began. As he worked more and more, he found a kind of comfort that would guide him in the future.

As an environmentalist, Sebastian could possibly restore what might have been wrong or prevent further damage to the planet. He would document everything he saw, meticulously study how each plant and animal interacted with the other, and then find a way to protect them both. Sebastian sought after the minute details in an environment to prevent the encroachment of man on the wilderness.

For example, Sebastian prevented a plastic factory from being built in Honduras, because of the mating habits of a frog, and was able to protect a huge section of his beloved rainforest in Panama by discovering an orchid unique to the whole of Central America.

The single discovery of the orchid would prove to be Sebastian's greatest accomplishment; at the same time, grant him opportunities for his future career and mark a significant change in the man.

* * *

The day I finished those journals, I cried again, and like the last time, I wasn't crying for myself; I was crying for Sebastian.

For years, Sebastian had pretended nothing mattered except his work. Like a dutiful husband and father, he went to work every day; never once did Sebastian let on as to how miserable he might have been. Meanwhile, I was constantly telling him what a terrible father he was, when all along he felt abandoned, alone.

In a short matter of time, I, too, would leave him.

Sebastian's heart has been broken so many times when he was so young. How could I tell him I was dying?

Now Sebastian had a family of his own, he would never abandon it, regardless of the circumstances. The man I married would be faithful to the end, because of what had happened to him before he met me. His convictions were stronger than mine; stronger than any man I'd known.

My life had been about my daughters before the diagnosis, and even more so afterwards. I was doing what I was supposed to do to protect them, and I did protect them. What I failed to realize was that, in doing so, I'd alienated Sebastian. My preparation, teaching and pushing the girls had become more important than the family as a whole. Sebastian turned to his work, not surprisingly; the one thing that had remained constant in his troubled youth, the place he turned to in crisis.

It must have appeared to Sebastian I'd forgotten he was their father. Anna and Carina were my children, but they were Sebastian's, too. He responded to the behavior I'd demonstrated. Having known a part of his history, I should have realized he might have felt rejected, but I wasn't able see past my own ambitions.

Devotion was the unhindered sled on the already slippery slope I would descend. I devoted every waking moment to my daughters, and forgot the rest of the world. I sacrificed all the things around me that made a woman be a better mother. I told myself I didn't need the individual things most women needed, because the girls were more important. I also found a place as some sort of martyr in how much I sacrificed for them, especially after the diagnosis. In addition to my self-sacrifice, I let fear and jealousy creep into my pitiful reasoning. No one person was good enough, I thought. I'd raised those girls on my own. Somewhere, in the back of my mind, I knew that wasn't true, but I managed to keep pushing it away. Then, the dream happened. I couldn't stand the thought of some strange woman taking care of *my* children. I wasn't sure Sebastian would re-marry, and I didn't want to take a chance. My ability to think clearly at the time had been sketchy, at best. The illness kept me fighting for a stronghold on my martyrdom. It was the one thing that was the key to this whole drama, so I had convinced myself. I clung to it with the passion of a heretic. I reasoned the fear and the jealousy were the fuel to keep me going, but they only made me do crazy things. I began to doubt myself and Sebastian. In the end, it drove me into his office that day where I found those damned journals.

Now that I knew the complete history, everything had to change.

I was terribly wrong. This was not Sebastian's fault.

Why was it so easy to look back and see where I'd been wrong? I couldn't change any of the events in the recent past. The only choice was to do something for Sebastian's future; a future for the family as a whole.

However, what could I do to help my family when I knew I wouldn't be there?

All along, I'd known what was necessary for my daughters: someone had to be there on a daily basis to help them cope with their new lives. However, who?

Moreover, who could Sebastian trust to help him?

* * *

As I prepared my grocery list, I mentally began another: those who would and who could help Sebastian.

Sebastian's parents topped the list; mine were dead.

I wondered, only for a moment, what my mother would have been like as a grandmother.

Sabine would want to help, I was sure, but she couldn't do it on a daily basis; she was already struggling with health issues of her own. She also lived in Bonn, more than ninety kilometers from Krefeld.

That left Rainer, whom Sebastian was no closer to than the day we married. They were very cordial to one another that day, but his father left almost immediately after the ceremony. I'd only seen him once since then. Still, I thought Rainer would help. However, he lived in Stuttgart, even further away: three hundred and forty kilometers.

Then there was Jesse, who didn't live in the same country. Despite what Sebastian thought of her, there was no doubt in my mind that Jesse would move mountain or molehill, lake or ocean, Heaven and Earth to do what she could.

Last on the list was Sebastian's brother, Dirk, who by far lived the closest and could help. The rift between the two brothers had not been completely repaired, and would not be in my foreseeable future. Sebastian wouldn't have accepted his help if it had been offered, and neither of us trusted Dirk's wife. Besides, they had three children of their own.

Trust!

Sebastian would have a very hard time trusting me if he found out I'd read his journals.

What had I done?

The supermarket was a welcome relief to contemplating that question any further. However, on the drive to, and the whole time I was in, the market, I felt as if I'd forgotten something. I'd checked the list more than three times already, and found it to be complete. What could I have missed?

The basket was full, and I was heading in the direction to pay when something caught the corner of my eye; a picture of an orchid on the cover of a magazine.

Then I became conscious of what I'd forgotten; my mental list had not been exhausted, and there was more reading to be done.

I left the supermarket with the basket still full. The drive home was too far to get the information I needed. What I was looking for could be found in another store: a book store. I was only meters away, as opposed to kilometers.

My feet couldn't carry me fast of enough, and I was winded when I arrived. However, the book I wanted was there. I took it from the shelf and looked at the cover while I caught my breath: *Our Orchid*, by Ty Walker.

I spent the remainder of the morning reading snippets of the first few chapters of something similar to Sebastian's journal.

Immediately afterwards, I raced home. As I came through the front door, I gave the shopping list to Mary, and told her I left a basket in the market; she might find it still there. I needed to be alone.

At the book store, my research was cursory. At home, I'd have the time to fully take in what Ty had written. Alone, once again, to uncover more of the secrets of my husband's checkered past.

Our Orchid was on the bookshelf in the living room. The book had been there for years; was Ty laughing at me the whole time?

Sebastian received the book before it came out. I'd never bothered to read it. I wasn't even sure Sebastian had, either. However, he must have. Why wouldn't he?

Ty's book was like reading *CliffsNotes* in addition to the book assigned for required reading; Sebastian's journals. It gave the important insights to what Ty and Sebastian had been experiencing. Initially, they'd both been documenters of a sort. Sebastian had been cataloguing plants and animals. Meanwhile, Ty had focused his writing on his feelings for Sebastian. Like two individual chords binding themselves together in silence, one was strengthening the other to face the world together.

Ty had written a moving description of two teenage boys finding more than strength, more than companionship; they'd found each other and they'd found love.

The juxtaposition of the characters in the book with Ty and Sebastian was not a difficult one. Some of the very things that took place in Ty's fiction, Sebastian had related to me on occasion. However, Ty was much more revealing in his written recitation of the same events.

As only a fiction writer could, Ty brought the daily routine of the characters, and what I'd imagined he and Sebastian had done, into a new light. Little things that would have been insignificant to most were bonding factors for the book's fictional characters, Ty and Sebastian. Who would have imagined how a simple exchange of music or planting trees could bind two people together? However, Ty found a way. Every word and deed delivered from the heart.

When I realized what Ty had meant to Sebastian in the past, my old jealous feelings rose to the surface like stale and trapped air; underwater far too long and just as quickly. Since Carina's birth, I'd had no real reason to doubt Sebastian's fidelity. Our relationship had moved into a comfortable place; a quiet surrender on both our parts.

I wanted to hate Ty, but found I couldn't. What had he done, after all? He'd always been more than pleasant to me and the girls. On the few occasions Ty had been to Germany, he brought us gifts. In short, he'd been the perfect gentleman.

However, that didn't stop me looking for reasons why I might come to hate him. I couldn't remember one slight, one flaw, not one minor infraction in the past, because there were none. Until recently, Ty never stayed at our house when he visited, which, of course, I wondered about. I thought it was a bit odd, especially since there was plenty of room. I didn't need to wonder any longer.

Perhaps the temptation was too great. I then asked myself if I would have been able to do what Ty had done for so long. There was no doubt in my mind Ty still loved Sebastian. Could I actively participate in the life of the man I'd loved for years and do nothing? Could I be friends with the women who had, in effect, taken that man from me?

The last time Ty was hear, he'd even confided in me about his latest relationship. I felt honored and trusted as a friend. I also remembered how easily I was spellbound by him. As I listened to Ty talk about some guy named Frank, something resonated inside me. The pleasure it gave made me want to agree with everything Ty had said. I hung on his every word. Instead of appreciating the words, I lashed out.

Not at Ty directly, but certainly in his direction. The feeling that I'd been laughed at for years unleashed an anger I couldn't control. I needed to demonstrate I still had some control over the situation. Give him something to keep him preoccupied while I figured out what I was going to do with this new information.

There was no way I could get to Ty without going through Sebastian, and, if I had tried to establish contact with Ty without Sebastian, it could raise questions I was not prepared to answer. How was I to get to Ty and continue to keep Sebastian in the dark?

Jesse!

* * *

"Hello, Jesse."

"Beatrice?"

"Why are you so surprised? I thought I'd call and preempt yours."

"I like the sound of that. Proactive women are my kind of women."

Was she psychic now, too?

"Well, I also have an ulterior motive."

"Even better! What can I do for you?"

"I need you to bring me something; when you come?"

"Sure, what would you like?"

"Some books."

"Books?"

"Yes, some books. I disagree with some of the translations in a couple of books we have in German and one that has yet to be translated. Before I make a mistake, I'd like to check the English versions to clarify a few things."

"Beatrice doing some research? I like the sound of that even more. Which books are we talking about?"

"*No Name in the Street* by James Baldwin, *Invisible Man* by Ralph Ellison, and *Our Orchid* by Ty Walker."

"Well, well! Mr. Walker just signed a new contract for his next book."

"Yes, I know!"

"How do you know that? It's not common knowledge."

"Jesse, he's one of Sebastian's oldest friends. You don't remember him at the wedding?"

Although I couldn't see Jesse's face, I knew the wheels were turning in her mind. I was sure, in a matter of time, she would ask me for an introduction. I had prepared something altogether different for her. I needed to stir up the pot a little.

"Not really; it must have slipped my mind. Otherwise, I would have asked you for an introduction long ago."

"Well, I might be able to do better than that for you."

"How so?"

"I don't know that I should be saying something to anyone, much less a journalist."

"Oh, tell! We have no secrets!"

I thought my husband had none from me.

"The last time Ty was here, we got a little drunk, and there may be trouble on his very near horizon."

"Really, go on."

"You have to promise you won't breathe a word. Sebastian and Ty would kill me if they found out."

"If you don't tell me now, I'll call every hour on the hour until you do."

Jesse hadn't promised, but I knew I had to keep going. I needed that promise from the journalist and my friend.

"Okay, okay! Ty's relationship with the current *beau* is in trouble. Ty denied it, but the *beau* suspects there's been an affair. Someone from Ty's past."

"Who could it be? Do you have any idea?"

"No, Ty wasn't that drunk."

"Don't hold back on me now; my mouth is salivating."

Prudence was an absolute necessity in dealing with Jesse. If I gave too much information rather quickly, she'd be suspicious; too little, and she might not chase the leads.

"There's no more to tell. That's all I know."

"For some reason, I'm not buying that."

"Honest, that's all I know."

"Well, I'm too curious now. This could be very good for me. If I could get the scoop on some very juicy gossip…"

"Jesse, you said you wouldn't."

"I'm not going to contact Mr. Walker. I'll call the boyfriend, and he can give me some suggestions. What's his name?"

Jesse could easily do the deed. All I had to do was give her Frank's unlisted number, and she would do the rest. She'd pester him until she got what she wanted. She never gave up. I'd have to give her some information to ask about, too, but I' was positive she'd manage the job perfectly.

"Bea?"

There was no quizzing inflection in her voice. Had she seen through another weak attempt to throw her off the track?

"Yes?"

"Bea?"

The slight tilt in her voice the second time was deafening. Not only had I managed to peak her curiosity, I'd been able to almost make Jesse forget to whom she was speaking. The need for information, the possibility of righting some wrong, and the knowledge she was inches away from the start of a hunt slipped Jesse into professional mode, and that was Jesse at her best.

"Yes?"

"You've come this far; give me the number."

"I can't; I've already said too much."

"Every half hour on the hour, and you know I'll do it."

"Fine, but this doesn't come back to haunt me, got it?"

"I promise."

* * *

With that promise, a new chapter began for all of us.

Soon enough, I'd know just how involved Ty was with my husband, past and present, and, as an added bonus, I'd get regular updates as opposed to daily health checks. I wasn't sure how Jesse would get the information. Nor was I really concerned. I assumed she would do what she has done in the past. None of the people Jesse had exposed liked her tactics. Somehow, I was sure neither would Ty.

Jesse had kept one secret so far as my girlfriend. She'd protect her source to the death, or at least until mine.

* * *

When I began reading Sebastian's journal, I was looking for answers. Where I'd failed myself was not asking the right questions. Then, after reading Ty's book, I was plagued by hundreds of them; questions and answers.

The majority of the questions, I would never have been able to ask Sebastian directly. To confront him was not an option. I would have to suffer in silence. Nothing could be done about the past, anyway. Part of me felt Sebastian's pain, and I was angry again. There was nothing I could do to keep either feeling in check. As the sympathy swelled and the anger receded, I was taken out of my rhythm and thoughts. In the end, I was forced to see all the sides of the story.

I had to go on, daily, carrying my own secret and, now, Sebastian's. Hopefully, he

66

wouldn't know how I'd betrayed him until after I was... gone.

All of the answers I'd found were to questions I'd never even thought about asking.

What I learned, however, gave me a way to give something to my family as a whole. It was easy for me to see that Sebastian was the man Ty had written about in the novel. Sebastian's characteristics had been copied to the letter. There were no physical or personal descriptions of Sebastian's friend in the journal. The question never occurred to me if Ty was 'the' friend.

Ty's novel was set in Central America. I knew they had traveled together; Sebastian had told me that. However, exactly where and, most importantly, when, had not been said. Sebastian and Ty were together when they were both experiencing difficult periods of their lives. This was a key element in the plot of the book.

Had I not read both, Sebastian's journal and Ty's book, I would have never pieced it all together.

Initially, I thought I was putting the pieces of a puzzle together, but, again, I was wrong. Pieces, yes, but it was not a puzzle.

Sebastian was about to go through another 'difficult' period in his life, and he would need someone he could trust and confide in again. Especially when he found out I'd betrayed him, which was inevitable.

There was only one person I knew Sebastian trusted as much as me, and only one person who loved Sebastian as much as me.

Ty's feelings for Sebastian caressed every page of the novel.

Then I was lost.

I imagined Ty reading his words to a captivated audience. His voice, a soothing and mellow baritone, tickled the ear, teasing almost. I saw crowds of people mesmerized by the even cadence, delighted and afraid at the thought of being made so vulnerable in public. I felt that vulnerability in my living room as I read Ty's book.

Yet, the sincerity in the words commanded my full attention.

* * *

Sebastian would have to change his life to become mother and father. Unless he had the right help. There was only one alternative in my mind. Another woman was out of the question for me. There was no guarantee Sebastian would go back to Ty; something I didn't want to necessarily see, either. Nor was it the alternative I would have preferred, but it had to become an acceptable changeover.

Could Sebastian have a future with anyone?
I knew Sebastian loved me and our daughters, but he'd been in love with Ty first. Why not again? Even if they didn't get back together, Sebastian would have some help. The length of time was entirely up to the two men.

Anything was possible, but I had to stick to things I could manage. I had to get them on the same continent first.

It would be a terrible shame for Sebastian to have to give up his work, but, if Ty was in Krefeld, Sebastian could still work. The change from New York City to Krefeld would seem unimaginable for Ty, but there was no better place to write. He didn't have to stay in the house if he chose not to, or if Ty and Sebastian couldn't make it work between them.

The apartment was still vacant; I could make sure it stayed that way for a while longer. Perhaps some needed repairs and some refurbishing with a few additions geared towards a certain writer's appeal. If Ty started writing in the apartment, maybe proximity would lead him to the house. This was all too much to speculate.

Could it be managed before I died?

The only thing I could do was to try to get them back together. If I succeeded, I would be doing something for all of my family. Ty had reluctantly become family in my eyes. Not only would my daughters receive what they needed, but I'd be giving Sebastian someone to trust again.

It all sounded too easy, but the reality was much more complicated. People in general were unpredictable; Ty and Sebastian, as individuals, probably even more so. How would Ty react? Could he deal with suddenly being thrust back into Sebastian's life? How would Sebastian feel about it? Had Sebastian felt anything for Ty since we'd been married, and, if not, would Sebastian be able to feel that way again?

Those questions couldn't be resolved without manipulating the two of them, but I wasn't above that, and wouldn't be around to know if it worked or not. However, Jesse would. Ty was the logical person to help, as Sebastian's best friend, and given their past. Jesse was not the most logical of choices, but she was mine.

However, Sebastian wouldn't allow her a daily role in the lives of our orchids. If Jesse and Ty helped, they'd hopefully have an equal amount of influence. Or I could put it in my will that way.

Sebastian, Ty and Jesse would read my will and learn my wishes, and, if necessary, Ty could tell the whole story to Sebastian far better than I.

Making my own will was the most practical way of getting all of them on the same page.

As godparents, Jesse and Ty could each have a certain amount of influence in the girls' lives. I was not sure Ty would agree without Jesse, and I was sure Jesse would be angry if I hadn't included her. I thought the two would complement each other very well; Ty, the romantic, and Jesse, the voice of reason. Sebastian might have agreed to Ty, but certainly not Jesse. I would have to make it decidedly clear I wanted both. Half the battle was over before it had started.

* * *

I was going over some of the beginning designs for helping the girls a week or so later when my playmate returned. This time, she was interfering with the chess game I was setting up for Anna. I wasn't aware of her presence until Anna said something.

As I placed each piece on the board, I was calling out their names… or so I thought I was.

"Mommy, what are you doing?" Anna asked me.

"I am showing you how to set up the board; this is the king…"

Sebastian.

"This is the queen…"

Beatrice

"This is the bishop…"

"I know. But the pieces don't have names like me and you. They have other names."

"You and…"

In midsentence, I realized I had been giving them the names of my family and associating them accordingly.

"She's right… but they can be manipulated, like pieces of the game," my playmate whispered.

* * *

A few hours later, after Anna's lesson, I ran with the suggestion. In my game of chess, the objective was a bit different: protect the king and the bishops at all costs, *and* win.

Also, in my game of chess, the rules of play had to be changed to suit me. I was out numbered and running out of time. I broke rules to equalize the disparity. None of the pieces had the faintest idea they were part of a game. Nor had they been aware I might not have been playing by any established rules. The pieces remained the same contemporary pieces, but their significance to me was very different.

Sebastian was the king; I was the queen.

My daughters were the bishops, represented by their innocence.

Ty was the knight: faithful to the king or the queen; limited moves, but never far from the king.

Jesse was the rook: faithful to the queen; the ability to move about in odd ways.

Trust, loyalty, information, lies, manipulations, wills, money, and words were all pawns. They were disposable, used against an opponent to win. These particular pawns were also disposable or necessary for the king or queen to survive the game. They were available to the king, but most often used only by the queen.

Ty and Jesse were duplicitous in their loyalties to either the king or queen, assuredly so in the past, presumably so in the present and, ultimately, in the future. Part of their loyalties would be divided at times, pulled in directions neither wanted to go, but needed to go, and parts of them sacrificed as a result. However, once the queen was gone, they would only have the king to aide in protecting the innocence of the bishops.

In this game, however, I was not only a piece, but a player, too. I chose, for all involved, what would be sacrificed, when, why and how. I had knowledge the 'pieces' didn't as a player. Given this knowledge, I was able to move the pieces about in whatever fashion I chose, to win at all costs, knowing that my fall as a piece could not be avoided.

* * *

While daydreaming one day, I saw an antique clock and my body merge. I could hear the minute hand ticking, *tick tock tick tock*, moving, advancing at a pace not controlled by the normal spring mechanism. This new mechanism, cancer, was in complete control, moving itself nearer and nearer to the end of my life.

Time became 'the' opponent sitting in the chair opposite me, skillfully maneuvering its pieces in order to gain the upper hand. Initially, I took a defensive posture. I was willing to sacrifice every pawn to simply hold ground. Then, my view would alternate: one view of the board from above, and then another from the vantage point of the queen on the board. From above, I could map my opponent's every possible move in advance. From the board, I kept a watchful eye on what was ahead of those who needed to be protected.

My opponent wasn't aware of the advantage I had been given in the minutes after the game began. Knowledge, however deceptively gained, would prove the key to my success or failure. Now that I knew what Sebastian had withheld from me in the past, I could direct the future with greater ease. Time would soon be on the defensive.

If I could control the flow of information in the future with my will, use the information of the past to my advantage, then all that was left was the present, and, although I might not have been able to control the information in the present, I did have the power to shape it. Trust, one of the first pawns to be sacrificed, opened many more views as to who the other pieces really were.

For instance, the knight would lose one of its two parts to protect the king. However, if the queen could persuade him to join forces, the loss would prove a benefit to the knight at the end of the game.

The rook, loyal to the queen, wouldn't necessarily need to be made aware of the queen's plans. Yet, she would defend the plan to the death once revealed. The rook, too, would have to lose a part of herself to play a different role in the future. Perhaps, in the future, the knight and the rook would, in fact, have a combined persuasive power over the king.

I'd lose the battle with time, but I'd win the war of protecting my daughters' futures.

The game had not just begun. Trust was the first pawn to fall, but there were still others to be held onto or relinquished, in time. Pawns, rooks, and knights could be lost – would be lost – to protect innocence.

The bishops, Anna and Carina, were innocent.

Innocence on their parts wouldn't presume guilt on the part of the others, but it wouldn't preclude it, either. There was at least one piece who will have felt the guilt, and another might think it had been thrust upon him, and spectators of the game might even say unjustly.

The fact of the matter was that we'd all made promises, verbal, implied and written, in marriage vows, births, and friendships. So, in fulfilling my promise of a better life for Anna and Carina, I was forcing the others into keeping their promises, too.

There were no guarantees, and my opponent was crafty. Chance was on my side, however. Knowing all the pieces as I did, there was a certain amount of assurance and guesswork on my part. I could manipulate their moves as the player, and participate as the play unfolded, as a piece. With the two vantage points, each unique in perspective, one common goal was shared – *win*.

Promise or not, game or not, life or death, the end result would be the same: the queen would fall. I, Beatrice Schütler, the queen, would take that fall when necessary. Until then, I'd play the game and move about as the queen pleased, cataloguing every move of the opponent and sharing that information as I saw fit.

I'd kept the pieces in the dark thus far, most not even aware of the game, much less being one of the pieces, including myself.

What did most people do when faced with their own mortality? I wasn't most people. I chose to play a game.

Or perhaps the game chose me.

Chapter 5

There was nothing to prolong my life as long as I would have wanted. I wanted to live to see old age, and, if not to old age, at least long enough to see my daughters' futures realized, maybe even see my grandchildren. However, that reality was not my reality: death was in my near future, as opposed to somewhere down the road.

Faced with the knowledge for almost a year now that I'd have a limited amount of time, I'd begun a journey. It was a lonely and cold road. Comfort was a thing of the past. There were times I wished I didn't have to carry this burden alone, but I wasn't sure this particular journey would have been easier or more comfortable for anyone other than me.

Even when faced with her own death, a woman's work was never done.

Given the right means, that work didn't need to be difficult.

Anger could be a great tool. Most of us were beaten over the head by it. We allowed anger to control us. Recently, I'd learned how to get a handle on mine. I wasn't always successful, but I did learn to bring it out in others to understand their true feelings. Sebastian was easy. Why was it so easy?

He loved me once; maybe because I knew him, almost every part of him. Despite my uncontrollable fear that our marriage was falling apart, we still remained friends, and I took advantage of his kindness. After years of marriage, I knew how to engage him. All I had to do was press him long enough on one subject, and he would finally admit any real reservations. Having arrived at his hesitation, we could discuss what the issue at hand really was. I hadn't done it consciously in the past. I learned to draw him out as an afterthought, actually. He followed the same pattern with almost every major decision we'd ever made.

Moving into my parents' house was one of those decisions.

We hadn't saved enough money for a down payment, and Sebastian was fixed against using the money my parents left me. He was also determined not to ask either of his parents for one cent. His mother lived as best she could. She didn't struggle; she simply had enough for herself. His father had more than enough, but he wouldn't dare ask him.

It took Sebastian a while, but he finally admitted the real reason. The house had been vacant since my parents died. It answered the question about a decent home, and we could use the money we'd saved for a better purpose. His reasoning was sound. The argument would have been easily won had he made his case, but I had to dig it out of him. The process took too long as to why he was so eager to persuade me.

What I failed to realize was that it had more to do with Sebastian's pride than anything else. I didn't recognize it, because he'd never truly exposed this side of him. He wasn't a proud person at all. However, since we'd been married and had a baby on the way, his focus had changed. He wanted to provide for his family.

We were already living in an apartment once owned by my parents, which took some getting used to on his part. My reasons for not wanting to move into the house were purely personal, and I was not vested in them. The move would help me put the past to rest. The house, other than my father's desk, had nothing to do with my feelings for my parents, and he was right; it would be a great place for the girls to grow up in. It was also a great opportunity to make some new memories.

Had I not pressed him, who knows where we might have ended up?
Then there was the decision about private school versus public school. His first objection was the distance from the house to the school. Again, he raised a valid point. If the girls went to private school, we'd also have to buy a new car. We would need something more reliable than what either of us had at the time. A new car was inevitable, I reminded him. His next objection was also summarily shot down and the next and the next. Finally, he came clean. Sebastian's real reason was fear that a private school might make us seem elitist and make our daughters spoiled.

I had no intentions of 'spoiling' our children. If all had gone as planned, they would have been the most well rounded children in Krefeld. However, I wasn't going to deny them anything. The money my parents left me was what was needed to guarantee the futures of both of them and take care of all of us in the process. At the time, nothing was more important to me. Frankly, I didn't care what anyone else thought. I had one purpose in life and, with that money, I had the means. I certainly was not going to waste the opportunity. It gave me great pleasure spending my parents' money on our daughters. I felt it somehow made up for all the things my mother and I did without.

By the time my last holiday with my family was being planned, I'd learned to employ the technique with a minimum of effort.

* * *

Like years before, Sebastian and I had planned our summer vacation months in advance. Everything had to be arranged around his schedule. My life and the lives of our daughters were fairly uncomplicated, but his crusades around the world took precedence over anything else. It annoyed me, at times, that I had to remind Sebastian he had a real family, too. Especially when he would try to coordinate our vacations with something he was currently working on.

"Our vacations should not be a working vacation for you," I'd argued many times. "Your children should have the opportunity to have your undivided attention on these trips, as opposed to when you are working."

Like many years in the past, Sebastian had suggested hiking. Normally, I would have argued against it. I would use the youth of the girls as an excuse, among other things, not to do so. However, this time, I said yes, as long as there were several concessions. The most important thing was we had to be near a hospital, in case of emergency, and not some hospital located in a small town, but near a hospital equipped for any real emergency. We also had to stay in Europe. This was stipulated so he would be less likely to try to work at the same time; few places in Europe had captured his attentions. Lastly, we should invite another family or friends to join us.

The last stipulation was mainly for the girls and me. I knew I was pushing the limits with the last request, but I left him an out. Sebastian wouldn't like going with another family; I knew that. I was hoping he would come up with an alternative we could both live with, and I tried to get him to suggest someone. Like a friend, perhaps a 'special' friend. I hadn't said that specifically, although I wanted to.

Of course, he missed the boat. Sebastian thought I was referring to some of our mutual friends with kids. They were my friends, not his, he'd said on many occasions. Sebastian had even thought I was referring to his coworkers. There were, among some of his colleagues, a group of people he could travel with, and often did, to various places they had sought to protect. I had to veto the idea. I didn't want his normal cohorts on our holiday. Not this holiday, anyway.

I made several more attempts to get Sebastian to think more along the lines of someone else, someone he had been on holiday with before. Someone we could both enjoy

75

being with. Still, Ty hadn't come to mind.

Finally, I suggested it to Sebastian. I found him in a particularly good mood one afternoon working at the dining room table. Normally, he worked in his study with the door closed as a clear indication he didn't want to be disturbed. However, this project needed more space than his desk could provide. He had been organizing several groups of slides.

"Sebastian, when was the last time you spoke to Ty?"

"It's been a while, as a matter of fact," he replied, without looking up from the slides.

"Did you ever think of asking him to go on holiday with us?"

"The thought crossed my mind, but I didn't think you would like it," he said, and looked up at me for my reaction.

"Why would you think that?" I retorted angrily. "We had a perfectly lovely time the last time he was here."

"You did?" he asked as he went back to his work.

"Yes, we did. As a matter of fact, he told me all about Frank and the problems they were having. I hope I was able to give him some good advice. We got a little tipsy that afternoon, but I think I was finally able to understand him," I replied, smiling to myself.

"What do you mean you hope you gave him some good advice? You didn't tell him he should stay with that guy, did you?" Sebastian asked, with more than a little irritation in his voice. He stopped his organizing and walked from the table to the window.

Well, well. I'd struck a nerve. The goal I was aiming for had produced something far more promising. I quickly surmised I wasn't the only one Ty talked to about his little problem. I didn't realize Sebastian would have this reaction. Why didn't he want Ty to be involved with this guy? Surely he didn't expect him to sit around and be lonely. However, I had to see where this was going to lead me.

"Well, not in so many words, no. I did say he should be sure the break up is what he wanted. And that sometimes love leaves us and comes to us regardless of the timing or the desires of those involved. Why? What did you tell him?"

"Oh Beatrice, that guy is all wrong for Ty. Besides, they were lovers once already, and it didn't work the first time. How do you suppose it will work the second time around? You shouldn't have told him that," Sebastian said.

"How do you know it won't work the second time around? Hopefully, this time he will go in having learned something he didn't know. Besides, we all need second chances sometimes to get it right. A chance to correct what went wrong in case we made regrettable mistakes."

"That's awfully romantic of you!" he said, with a little sarcasm in his voice. "But I think you are wrong about them. I think Ty needs to move on."

"Why?"

"Because I just don't think he's the right guy for him," he said; this time, he looked a little reminiscent. He stared off in the distance, searching for something or someone he had once known, I supposed.

Here was where I should have let sleeping dogs lie, but, of course, I didn't. Who was the right guy for Ty in his mind, and how would he know this? After all, they were not as close as they had once been. Or was he trying to say something to me? Was Sebastian the right guy for Ty? I was angry now, and it was my own fault.

"Who is the right guy, then?"

"I don't know, Bea, I don't know," he said as he went back to what he was doing.

Sure you do. Or are you just not willing to say it?

"But you seem pretty certain this guy is not the right guy. How is it you are so certain?" I continued. I knew I was pushing the envelope.

"Because I know Ty too well, much better than most," he replied. "And I'd rather not see him hurt again."

"I am sure you wouldn't," I said. It was my turn for a hint of sarcasm.

The words had slipped from my tongue as casually as goodbye or hello. My anger had let the words escape me. For a moment, I hesitated before looking at Sebastian. Fortunately, he'd continued with what he'd been doing. I was glad Sebastian hadn't caught the sarcasm in my voice.

I had to give up before my anger got the best of me. If I'd said any more, I wouldn't have been able to stop. If I'd said any more, I would have risked divulging what I knew. Then I would have had to explain how I knew these things. Like how he had wanted to protect Ty years ago.

After all these years, Sebastian was still trying to protect him. It didn't matter that Ty was years older and didn't need protection now, nor then. It didn't matter that Sebastian was married and had a family. That need to protect him was still present. What else was still there? The verbal sparring was over for now. I assumed there were many things the both of us were

77

alluding to, but neither of us would have said. Not outright, not at that moment. If we had, it would have been like a direct hit to the heart. I certainly wasn't ready for directness. I liked the dance, the strikes and the near misses. The game was all I had to live for now; I couldn't let it end before it had started, but, even more than that, I couldn't risk tipping my hand or losing. What had just happened would have to be chalked up to a near miss. I still had to convince him to invite Ty to come on holiday with us.

"Well, regardless of Ty's relationship problems, I think this would be a good distraction for him. And you know how the girls love him. Well, Anna does, anyway. I am not so sure about Carina. But I think you should call him and ask him. At least give him the opportunity to say no for himself."

"Fine, I will. But don't get your hopes up. He has a new book coming out, and I am almost sure he will be promoting it. Are you sure this is what you want?" he asked.

"I am sure," I replied, a bit perplexed.

How did he know about the new book? I had been looking, from time to time, at Ty's website, and there was only a small blurb about the new book. Of course he'd told us about it, but he was still sketchy about a date of publication. Was it possible my husband had been keeping more secrets? He said he hadn't spoken to Ty in a 'while', whatever that meant. If that was the case, how did he know this bit of information?

For the next few days, Sebastian was a little down. When I commented on it, he feigned fatigue. However, I knew differently. He had called Ty the very afternoon we discussed inviting him. I'd gone to his study to ask him a question, and the door wasn't completely closed. I wasn't eavesdropping, I told myself. I could hear him talking, so I hesitated for a moment. I heard Sebastian say 'it was Bea's idea to invite you'. When I heard him say that, I walked away. I could only determine, later, the response had been negative. He never mentioned calling Ty that day.

By the third or fourth day of watching him mope around the house, I decided to ask him again. He was sitting with Carina and Anna, pretending to be interested in the video the girls were watching. This was the best time to ask, because I could also see what the girls thought of Ty joining us. We hadn't discussed anything with them, and I was a little curious as to how they would react.

"Have you spoken to Ty yet about going on holiday with us?"

"We are going on holiday with Uncle Ty?" Anna asked as she sprang to her feet.

"When?"

Sebastian looked at me with disdain. However, I was happy to see Anna so excited. Carina was non-responsive.

Once Sebastian got over his anger, he'd finally said what I'd thought.

"I'm sorry, *mein Schätzchen* Uncle Ty can't come with us. He will be working," he replied.

Anna's happiness turned into dejection as quickly as it had come. She loved Ty more than anyone in the room, I thought. She was always happiest before and during his visits and a little sadder after he'd departed. My heart went out to her. It was clear she was having her first crush on the opposite sex. I wanted to pick her up and hold her. Two things prevented me from doing so: I didn't have the strength, and she exited the room before I was able to.

Tick, tick, tick.

Loss of strength was one of the symptoms. Anna was a little big for her age, but I still should have been able pick her up if I'd been healthy. As the cancer progressed, I would lose more and more of my normal strength. It wasn't permanent at this stage; the weakness came and went. Little things like this were constant reminders of just how little time I had. Having witnessed Anna's disappointment, I had to do something. She would be the key to Ty's success in the future; her help would be dire in dealing with Carina when I was… gone.

"Sebastian, would it help if I talked to Ty?"

"Bea, he said he has to work. I am not sure there is much either of us can do," he replied, with a touch of what was almost anger in his voice.

"In any case, I'd like to try."

"Fine, his number is on my cell phone. I think it's in the address book in my study, too. Knock yourself out. Just don't harass him about it, okay," he said.

"I won't harass *him*. Trust me."

Sebastian had merely dangled the bait, almost tiptoeing around the issue. I wasn't about to fail. This was a crucial point in the game, and far too early for any recalcitrance from Ty, or my husband, for that matter. If Ty waffled here, my job would only become more difficult in the future, and I didn't have the time or energy to fight a long battle. So, it was up to me to land the fish.

More importantly, there was a bit of information reconnaissance I had to do. The advice I'd given Ty wasn't meant for the two of them to get back together. I'd said what I'd said to gently steer Ty away from Frank. I'd figured, from various points in our conversation, Frank wanted to get back together more than Ty. Had my little ruse worked? My mind had been racing for months as to the outcome. If Ty had gone back to Frank, there would be trouble for me. Then I'd have to find a way to come between them, and, even though it would have been downright evil, I would have done it. However, I was putting the cart before the horse. *Let me find out what has happened and then go from there.* So, what reason should I have for calling?

* * *

"Hello, may I speak with Ty Parker?"

"Beatrice, is that you? This is Ty," he said.

"Yes, Ty, it's me; how are you?"

"I'm fine. What a pleasant surprise! How are you? How are the girls?"

He hadn't asked about Sebastian. Why?

"We are all fine, thanks. Listen, I just called to check up on you. The last time you were here, you said you were in the process of negotiating the new book deal. How's it going?"

"Great, Beatrice, thanks for asking. It's almost a done deal, actually. I start a limited tour in June, if all goes well," he replied.

"If all goes well; I thought you just said it was a done deal," I insisted.

"Well, you know how life goes, things come up that can't be helped. There are a few months between now and then; just trying to take one day at a time."

"Hmm, Ty, that sounds a little ominous coming from you; are you sure you are okay? This doesn't have anything to do with that Frank guy?"

"Very intuitive of you, Beatrice; as a matter of fact, it does. I am in the process of looking for a new place. I've been seeing places just about every day, packing and getting things moved to storage."

"Oh, Ty, I am sorry it didn't work out. I have been wondering how it was going. Is there anything Sebastian and I can do for you?"

"Not right now, Beatrice, but thanks for asking. It means a lot."

"Well, you know you always have a home with us. And, if you need a quiet place, you could come and stay at the flat we own. I'm sure Sebastian wouldn't mind at all. I can ask him if you'd like."

"That's very kind of you, Bea, but it's not necessary. I need to get myself settled here in New York. But, if things change, I will let you know."

"Well, I have a favor to ask of you."

"Anything for you guys."

"Ty, would you please come on holiday with us in June? I'm afraid the girls and I will be a bore for Sebastian. He needs another man on this trip. I'm also afraid if you don't come I'll have to do something with him like fishing."

"Bea, I'd love to come, I really would. But I can't get out of the appearances I've already scheduled. I told Sebastian the other day if the dates were further into the summer, there'd be no problem. My publisher will not be happy if I don't make the dates already set. You understand, don't you? I got the feeling Sebastian didn't in our last conversation."

That's why he hadn't asked about Sebastian. Did they have words?

"Of course I understand. I'll see what I can do on this end. I'll speak to you in a few days. By the way, what dates are you free?"

"Anytime after the third week of July and before Labor Day works for me, but that only gives us about five or six weeks. And, if we are going to do this, we have to book it soon. My publisher seems to be adding dates every other day. Oh, and Bea, thanks for inviting me. Sebastian said it was your idea," he said.

"It's nothing, Ty, you are always welcome! But listen, you would be doing me and the girls a big favor if you could come. I'll call you in a day or two."

Tick, tick, tick.

Well, that went over well. The only good thing to come out of that conversation was that the Frank character was out of the picture, which was one less worry to contend with, but why was it, lately, I was batting a thousand, but not in the direction I was aiming, and why hadn't Sebastian mentioned it was only a matter of changing the dates? No bother; the ball was in my court now. Could I easily persuade Sebastian to change the dates? Would there ever be an appropriate reason? I supposed I'd have to find one. First, however, I needed to get his schedule and see what the conflict was.

* * *

The next day, I was anxious about getting a look at his calendar, but I had to get him out of the house to have the proper amount of time to do the research I needed to do. What could I do? It was a Saturday, I think, and he had been in and out of his study all day.

What if I cooked this evening?

Perfect! I could send Sebastian to the store for some ingredient I didn't have. I could also ask him to take the girls by the bakery for their favorite deserts. That would give me enough time. The bakery and the supermarket were on opposite sides of town. Surely, he wouldn't deny the girls. It was up in the air as to whether or not he would deny me, and, inevitably, he would find an excuse to stop in at his office. His office was in between the two. If he did that, I'd have more than enough time.

"Carina, where are you?"

I knew she would be in earshot. She was hardly ever away from me. Sometimes I wondered if she had some special power and was aware of my illness. She seemed to be especially clingy of late, almost underfoot. There were days when all I needed was to look at her and know that what I was doing was well worth it.

"I am just here, Mommy," she said as she came walking into the kitchen. "I wasn't far."

"Carina, honey, can you do Mommy a favor?"

"Yes, Mommy, what is it?"

"Mommy needs something from the store. Can you ask Daddy to go into town and get me some cheese for dinner? I want to make Daddy's favorite tonight, and we don't have any cheese. And ask him to take you by the bakery. You and Anna can choose your favorite desserts."

"Can we get anything we want?" she asked enthusiastically.

"Of course you can!"

"Daddy, Daddy! Mommy said we can get anything we wanted. Daddy, where are you?" she called.

The one thing I wanted to avoid in my little game was using the girls, but, inevitably, they would be dragged into the adult drama. They were the only 'equipment' I had to play with. I hated using the girls to do my work. The least I could do was keep them directly out of the game. So, I limited their roles. After all, tennis can't be played without a net, right? Even though it simply stands there, it had a purpose. The net occasionally had an impact on the outcome of the game. The girls, too, had a purpose, at this point, and an impact that was more than occasional.

The ruse to get Sebastian out of the house was also a sort of training. There would be times in his near future when he would have to run such errands. When shoes were forgotten at school or lunch was left behind, for instance. Those little inconveniences would have to be attended to. It was better Sebastian practiced now, and I needed to get into his office, where he'd been all day.

I didn't need permission, this time, to go into his study; not that it had stopped me before. As I headed to down the hallway, I suddenly stopped short of the door. The last time I was in his study, I'd read those journals. Then my world had almost turned upside down. Then I was the wounded animal waiting for death to come to me. It was amazing how much had changed in a few months. All of a sudden, I was the hunter instead of the hunted. I'd told death I wasn't going quietly. My reluctance did surprise me for a moment, however, but then I shook it off and went about what I'd planned to do. The calendar was in plain sight on his desk.

* * *

Once I got Sebastian's schedule, the next step was to talk to Dana. Dana knew Sebastian's schedule better than he did. The key here was to get Dana to check to see if whatever the conflict was could be rescheduled. I had to do this in case Sebastian said 'I'll have to check with Dana'.

Then I could say I'd already checked with her and there were alternative dates. Otherwise, I'd have to come up with something on my own, or perhaps another lie. Would one more lie really have made a difference at that point?

"Why should I have to do all the little things?" I asked myself.

I had to stay one step ahead of all of them if this was going to work.

* * *

There were two conferences and two presentations on Sebastian's calendar. I figured the conferences couldn't be rescheduled, but the presentations were completely incumbent upon Sebastian. Ty had only a five- or six-week period to work with.

The stunt I'd pulled a few days ago proved more than helpful. Not only did I have enough time to snoop, but I was able to make notes as to his plans for the coming weeks. Sebastian was going to Berlin soon. That trip would give me the opportunity to speak to Dana about making changes in his schedule.

* * *

"Dana, this is Beatrice."

"Oh, hello, Beatrice; what can I do for you?"

"I need you to tell me if one of Sebastian's presentations could be rescheduled. I'd like to schedule our vacation for the second and third weeks in August, and he has a presentation scheduled for the third week. Could you call them and inquire about alternative dates?"

For a moment, I felt as if I'd put Dana in an awkward situation. I had never actively interfered in Sebastian's work life. The thought had never occurred to me. In all the time that we'd been married, his work had been first, but, now, things were different. I didn't care that I'd crossed the line. Not only had I jeopardized the vacation, but I'd dragged unsuspecting Dana in the midst of a game that was not meant to involve her.

I reasoned to myself that the excuse Sebastian gave was not good enough. Time was too precious a commodity. Everyone seemed to have it but me. I hadn't even thought of what might happen to Dana if Sebastian were to become angry. Surely he'd be able to understand. If not, I'd tell him it was my doing, and to hell with the rest.

"Any alternative dates in particular?" Dana asked.

"No, so long as they don't conflict with anything else Sebastian has scheduled, but call me first with the new dates."

"Sure, I'll call them tomorrow," Dana said, a little distressed.

Dana had wanted to call the next day for a reason. It's possible she'd felt something was not quite right, but, overall I knew she wanted to run my plans by Sebastian. I'd heard the slight hesitation in her voice. There was only one person to whom she had to be loyal. Had I been in Dana's place, I would have done the same thing, but I wasn't. The time to act had been determined by the lack of enthusiasm of Sebastian and Ty. I was the only one willing to face up to what had to be done. I couldn't wait for the two of them to work it out in their own time.

"Could you call today, please? I'm trying to arrange a special surprise for Sebastian, and I need to know today, if possible."

"Okay, I'll call you as soon as I have some suggestions."

"Thanks, Dana, and please don't mention this to Sebastian."

"Okay, I won't," she said.

Next, I had to call Ty and check those dates with him.

"Hello, Ty, I know you must be busy, so I'll be quick. How are the second and third weeks in August?"

"Those dates are fine," Ty said.

"Pencil us in, then. Sebastian has a possible conflict, but we are working on changing it. May I ask another favor?"

"Anything for you," he said.

"Can you keep this between the two of us? I'd like to surprise Sebastian with the news, if this all works out."

"Sounds good to me."

"Great, thanks, Ty. I'll call you if anything changes."

I felt a sense of pride about what I had accomplished that day. Dana had called back and said there were, in fact, alternative dates for the presentation. Ty had penciled in the dates in August. All was well!

* * *

The final stage in this part of my little game was set in motion. Or so I'd thought, anyway. When Sebastian returned, things were not so set in stone.

Dana had called Sebastian to give him a heads up as to what I was trying to do. I could tell from the way he came in the door something was wrong. Normally, he spoke when he came into the house. Not only didn't he speak, he went straight to his study. I didn't have to wonder why.

Immediately, I began to prepare my defense. Was there really anything to defend,

85

however? We all needed this vacation. I was not about to feel guilty for doing what was right for all of us, finally. Surely Sebastian had to see this, and, even if he didn't, I'd make him see it. It might have been a little late in the game, but I was not going to play second fiddle to his job on this particular occasion. Besides, what was the harm in postponing one of his damned presentations?

The girls and I had put our lives on hold for Sebastian's career on far too many occasions. Birthdays, concerts, school plays, all taped so he could see what he'd missed. Well, this was one event that couldn't be taped, and his presence would be required. This trip held far more significance than he could have imagined. Too much planning had gone into this vacation to let him interfere. If he had done what he was supposed to and convinced Ty to join us on the trip, we wouldn't have been in this situation.

The planning of my defense was sounding more and more like a battle of wills; mine against Sebastian's. No matter what he said, I had to win the argument. However, I also felt the anger mounting within. I had to get myself together before he started his tirade. My diplomacy skills were a bit rusty of late, however. These were not the ingredients of a good start to win a persuasive argument, and, with the stakes as high as they were, Sebastian had to be convinced beyond reason. This vacation was going to happen.

The success or failure rested firmly in my hands. I was right and angry, but the combination wasn't always good for me. I needed this win based on my ability to argue. My latest little victory had been managed by manipulating dates and events; hardly very competitive. However, with this encounter, there was a greater sense of competition, and this was what competing was all about, no? Taking on your opponent, one on one, and using the contest to come to the understanding of who was the better of the two. The sad thing was that my adversary was my husband.

Perhaps I shouldn't have been so aggressive after my last win. Perhaps I shouldn't have argued. Then again, maybe I'd been looking for a fight.

Since reading the journals and Ty's book, I'd remained the happy homemaker I'd always been. To the whole of the household, nothing had changed, least of all me. I was still Mommy and wife, fulfilling all the duties and functions required of each, but I had, in fact, changed. Somewhere inside me, the bad girl was demanding the same attention as Mommy and wife. The bad girl wanted equal billing, and this was her opportunity to prove she could hold her own.

* * *

Deep in thought, I didn't hear Sebastian come down the stairs. When he came into the kitchen, he had his calendar in his hand.

"Do you want to tell me what's going on?" he asked.

"Well, I asked Dana to change one of your presentations."

"Yes, I know that. The only question remaining is why," he said angrily.

"It was supposed to be a surprise."

Don't get angry, I said to myself. *Let him state his case, and then pounce on him afterwards.*

"Beatrice, you know I don't like surprises, especially when it involves changes in my schedule. What gives?" he asked again.

Surrender was the next thought. Let him feel as if he'd won. This was going to make it easier for all concerned. Pounce, surrender, pounce, surrender; my mind vacillated back and forth for a minute.

"Oh, all right! Ty and I have arranged some dates so he could come on the trip with us."

Sebastian stood there for a moment, looking at me as if I'd struck him in the face; a complete look of bewilderment. However, I couldn't understand why. Was he angry? Was he surprised I'd accomplished where he had failed? I thought he would be happy about this. The look on his face was not the look of happiness. Instead, it was the look of doubt, and maybe a little frustration. What had I done wrong? I had asked him if I could try to convince Ty to come with us, and his response had been yes. So what was the problem here?

"What's gotten into you lately?" Sebastian asked. "You are going behind my back to make changes in my schedule. You've never done that before. Something is not right. What's going on, Bea?"

The accusation of going behind his back was too much. In my mind, I had done *no* such thing in terms of this vacation. What I *had* done was exert more of my own influence in an area of our lives I had never meddled in before, and I was losing the battle of being patient.

"What's going on, you ask? I'm tired of being last on your list of things to do. The girls and I are your family, and we deserve to have this vacation. You're right! I've never interfered in your work, and I am just now realizing I should have done so long ago. We are having this trip, with or without you. Ty has a limited amount of time, and I wanted to make sure this was done."

"Did you stop to think maybe Ty wasn't the person I'd have chosen to go with us?" Sebastian asked.

"Then why didn't you stop me from calling him?"

"Because he said no the first time. I didn't think he would change his mind, to be honest."

"Sebastian, he said he told you the dates were wrong for him. Why didn't you say something?"

"Because I have obligations: conferences, presentations, and not much time in the summer. I didn't want to make changes to the schedule," he answered aggressively.

"Well, I am sorry; the dates have been confirmed," I replied in anger.

Tick, tock, tick, tock.

There was so much more I wanted to say about *his* time and *his* schedule. Now was not the time to get into a big argument about things I should have addressed years ago. Now was the time to give in and win this battle. There would be plenty of time, and much more of a war to fight, very shortly, I was sure.

"Listen, I know I should have talked to you first. But then it wouldn't have been a surprise. I didn't want you to be bored, and thought having Ty along would be a good thing for you," I tried to explain.

The small retreat worked. The look on Sebastian's face became less confrontational. "I appreciate what you're trying to do. I'm just not sure Ty is still the hiking guy anymore. I think four-star hotels are more his style of holiday now," he said.

The sound in his voice reminded me of the journals. For a split second, the image of him alone on the beach flared in front of me and made me a little gentler.

"He didn't seem to have a problem with it when I told him what we were doing."

"Fine! It's no big deal. But I still think you're up to something. Am I wrong?"

"The cat's already out of the bag. There is nothing more to tell."

Sebastian tuned and walked away.

The last of the lies?

Why doesn't he want Ty to come on this trip? The four-star hotel thing is a bad excuse.

I can see through that. What is the real reason?

Is Sebastian still trying to protect Ty, or is he trying to protect himself?

Did it matter who he was trying to protect? In either case, something was there. Something Sebastian was willing to guard for all eternity, and, like writing in his journals, he'd have much more time when I was… gone.

* * *

In the end, all of us made additional compromises about the vacation. Sebastian reluctantly changed his schedule. Ty changed the dates once more, but they worked in Sebastian's favor, so that was fine. Ty also suggested we do a combination hike and cabin trip, which suited the girls and I. We wouldn't have to be in tents for too long.

Sebastian also changed the location, but no one seemed to care. I certainly didn't. Where we were wasn't the reason for the trip. Two other reasons were much more important. I needed to see the two of them together again. My imagination had run wild long enough. If there was still something there, I wanted to witness it for myself to assure this was truly going to work.

In addition, there was a surprise of my own I had for the two of them.

* * *

The initial interaction between Ty and Sebastian was almost comical. I stood back and watched from a distance. I could not hear what they were saying, but I felt the tension. Ty told me what happened later on:

"Do you still remember how to pitch a tent?" Sebastian asked me.

He'd almost read my mind. It wasn't hard to see I was having a problem. I hadn't forgotten. I was just out of practice.

"Of course I do!"

I couldn't let Sebastian outshine me.

"I was afraid success had made you soft," he said.

"Not to be cliché, but it's like riding a bicycle. You never forget."

"Oh really! You seem to have forgotten everything else," he stated angrily.

What was he doing? Why was Sebastian trying to provoke me? What was he so angry about?

"What's that supposed to mean?"

"Forget I said it. That knot you are tying will not hold," Sebastian said with a smirk.

From the start, they bickered. The tension was so fantastic I thought one of them would be dead before the holiday was over, but, by the third night, they'd almost become friends again. They weren't quite where I wanted them to be, but they were at least talking to one another in a civil manner. That's when I started to try to direct the conversations. I had to make them both take a stroll down memory lane. Neither of them was headed that way on their own. So I tried to give them a little help.

"I'm sure this is less rustic than Panama."

By the looks on their faces, I'd found the right path.

They both broke into smiles and started telling the tales I had heard over and over. In a matter of minutes, they talked as if there were the only ones there. The girls had already gone to bed, and I decided to let them have a moment.

"Well, I am off to bed; good night, Ty," I said with a little smile of my own.

"Good night, Bea," Ty replied.

"Sebastian, there's a bottle of rum in the trunk of the car if you two want a drink. Tomorrow, I'll need to drive into town to pick a few things. Carina is out of muesli. I'd thought I'd packed enough, but I didn't. And you know how she gets if she doesn't have it. Should I get some beer, as well?" I asked.

"None for me, thanks. I'll stick to rum," Ty said.

"None for me, either," Sebastian said.

The rum was a last-minute addition. In his journals, Sebastian had written they drank a great deal of it. It was supposed to be in case of an emergency. As far as I was concerned, it had been perfect timing. In our tent, I listened to the two of them talking for a few hours. The stories they relived brought them closer; for one night, anyway. This part of the plan was working. As I thought about the day's events, I knew that all Ty and Sebastian needed to make things seem right again was a few hours alone, without the girls and me.

While we were camping, I saw what I'd brought us together to see, and probably a great deal more than what I'd wanted. The love Ty had so carefully written about made itself manifest, even when they argued. I watched from a distance like in the dreams, and felt it from meters away. As Ty was telling me what happened between them, I could see the constant devotion he'd held for my husband. I witnessed the lover, the friend and the muse. Ty probably wasn't aware of how Sebastian changed, but I was. Ty had become Sebastian's muse on the trip, and they fell into a rhythm they'd briefly shared before me.

I wasn't happy, but what could I do? My time was at its end.

However, the lives of our daughters were just beginning. No two people would be more willing to make amends to one another. As they cared for my daughters, each day would give them a unique opportunity.

The jealousies I'd felt before were not only about other women. Something else had kept Sebastian dedicated to his work. I had never asked, because I was afraid of knowing the truth. At first, I had thought it was something better than me, but that wasn't it at all.

Before I fell asleep, I realized it was a combination of two things. The solace Sebastian experienced while he worked was comforting to him. So he went there, time and time again, because he couldn't find it in people. It wasn't only 'something' in the end; it was someone. He ran to Ty when he ran into those remote places, secluding himself with those feelings from so long ago. Reliving the moments Sebastian shared with Ty kept him in that world and gave him the ability to live in this one.

* * *

The next morning, Sebastian asked me if it was absolutely necessary for the trip into town. I stated, without the least bit of hesitation: yes. The drive into town was essential to the surprise in store for both of them.

"You know how Carina gets without her muesli," I added.

No one knew I'd hidden the muesli, but there was so much none of them knew. Why should this be any different?

The alcohol had worn off, and the day would be a hard one for the two men. They would have to figure that out for themselves. Like so many things in their near futures. Neither knew that the future I was about to present to them would start so soon. As I prepared the things for the girls' outing for the day, I thought about my plan to finally tell Sebastian I was dying. The accident had to happen while we were on holiday, so that Ty was present. They would both find out at the same time, and I would not have to say the words.

* * *

The preparations for the accident had not been easy.

Dr. Koenig had told me how to maintain my health: what would happen if I consumed too much alcohol, and things to avoid in general. He had also informed me of the dangers of mixing my medications with simple over-the-counter medications. Even then, I was curious as to the effect it would have, but he wouldn't elaborate. I supposed he was concerned I might try something ill advised.

Jesse, once again, came to the rescue. I casually brought up the subject of mixing medications and, in true form, she slipped into reporter mode. Within an hour after talking to her, I received an email detailing the risks. She had even included several links to websites where I could get more information. What would I have done without my friend?

Yet, with all the resources she had made available to me, the best bit of information came from another source.

Most over-the-counter meds come with a pamphlet. Of course, this information was provided to limit the liability of the drug manufacturer. However, I was not concerned with their liability. I had only read the pamphlet in passing, but found what I had been looking for.

I had to purchase medication for Anna. She sometimes suffered from allergies, so I found a mild antihistamine. As I was reading the pamphlet, the medication I was taking to stop the fainting was one of the drugs listed that could cause a negative reaction. Immediately, I was intrigued. This particular antihistamine could raise the blood pressure. I remembered then that Dr. Koenig had said high blood pressure sometimes occurred and that my fainting could have been a result.

In my mind, the danger was minimal, but, in reality, the danger could have been fatal. If I took too much, it could create a bigger problem than I was willing to risk, and I would not get the desired effect. There was only one way to be sure. I had to test the dosage.

This little experiment was carried out one day at home. I asked the housekeeper to go into town for a few things. She'd be gone for most of the morning, but back soon enough in case I had complications. I took the antihistamine and waited for what seemed hours. Nothing happened. I was furious. I got up to look for the pamphlet, and I went right out.

The desired effect had been achieved.

The experiment lasted only a couple of hours. I was a bit groggy afterwards, but well enough to perform the normal duties of the day. Perhaps it was dangerous, far too dangerous, to play with drug interactions so casually, but I was running out of time. With each day, I felt as if I was losing more and more of myself. Fortunately, I'd only have to repeat this part of the game one more time.

* * *

As I started the trip into town, a feeling of relief settled on me. For so long, I'd lived in a continual state of fear of being found out; in a matter of hours, that fear would be gone. A load would be lifted from my shoulders, and I could carry on with the remainder of the game almost in the open. Some things would still require a bit of secrecy, but the diagnosis would become public domain, and, with each passing mile into town, I knew this phase of the game would bring into focus, for everyone, what I had worried about the most: my daughters.

The plan had been to drop off the girls at a nearby day camp, make a pit stop along the way to take the antihistamine, drive into town, and have my little episode in the supermarket.

There was a rest stop in between the town and the trail where we camped. I'd stop there, take the antihistamine, and then continue into town. The drive from the rest stop into town was less than twenty minutes. I'd have plenty of time to make it into town and into a supermarket so that, when the drugs took effect, I'd be in a safe place.

That's not what happened.

Tick, tock, tick, tock.

I made it to the pit stop and took the medication. However, as I got back on the highway, I had not driven more than several kilometers before I had to stop. The road to town was blocked for some reason. I couldn't see around the traffic. My nerves were already on edge. I was losing time.

As I sat impatiently in the car, the second dream came rushing forward.

At the start of the dream, I was in the car listening to my father go on and on about the price of something. My mother sat there with nothing to say; she simply looked out the window. All of a sudden, the interior of the car started to fill with smoke, but neither of them reacted. How could they not notice it?

Then I was standing on the highway at the exact point where the accident happened.

There were only two vehicles on the road: my parents' car and the transport truck.

Next, I was in the cab of the truck, sitting beside the driver. The man was asleep. I tried to grab the steering wheel to move the truck back onto his side of the road, but my hands were once again air thin. As I looked up, it was already too late.

Then everything went black.

The sound of the ambulance approaching startled me into reality. My mind snapped and thought of the antihistamine. I got out of the car. I didn't want to cause another accident. Walking towards the scene, I began to smell gas and burnt flesh like in my dream. The smoke above the car resembled the smoke in my parents' car.

I went out.

* * *

The second time I woke up in the hospital, I knew exactly why. A nurse was by my side, injecting something into my IV fluid. "How do you feel, Mrs. Schütler?"

"Very groggy."

Once I was sitting up properly, she went for the doctor.

My earlier preparations included this part of the accident, too. In my handbag, I'd brought a copy of the report I had received from my latest MRI. I was prepared to show it to the doctor, get him to read the findings, and ask him to tell me what it had meant. That wasn't necessary.

"Mrs. Schütler, I'm Dr. Lorenz. How are you feeling?"

"A bit groggy, but fine, otherwise."

"Mrs. Schütler, you received a head injury as a result of passing out at the scene of a car accident on the highway. Can you tell me what happened?"

94

"Well, I got out of my car to see what happened, and then, I'm here."

"I see; well, the paramedics informed us you fell onto a stationary car. As you were unconscious and had a head injury, we were obliged to do an x-ray and a MRI."

I almost stopped listening, because I knew what he was going to say.

"We found these tumors, and I am sorry to have to tell you this, but…"

Then the tears flowed.

To the doctor, it must have appeared natural when receiving such information.

However, to me, they were tears of relief.

This doctor, not our family doctor, was the one to say to my husband what I didn't have the courage to say. In this setting, far from home and possible recognition at our local hospital where I'd been getting some treatments, both men involved in my little game were alerted at the same time. Sebastian and Ty were the first to hear that poor Beatrice was dying. It was for these two men I'd done what I'd done. They would have to find a way to guard what I wanted to protect most, Anna and Carina, my daughters.

I'd decided a long time ago to make a game of it, because it helped me to sleep at night. If the game was played out right, one of my final acts, then I could say I'd done what a mother was supposed to have done. Game or not, the end result was all that mattered.

* * *

Jesse was the only one who heard the words from my own two lips. However, I couldn't say when exactly we'd had the conversation or where. The confusion was happening more frequently now, the lapses longer and longer.

The only woman I knew well was Jesse.

However, Sebastian hated her. Maybe 'hate' was a strong word. If there was any one person he disliked the most, it would have been Jesse. Strangely enough, I had the same reaction to her when we first met in university. I thought she was arrogant and silly until I got to know her. Jesse proved to be a loyal friend once we were in different classes. She still had the capacity to annoy people like she had then, but she had grown into a lovely person over the years. In my opinion, she had only one small flaw.

I had seen her play the helpless woman all too often, and this was something I certainly didn't want my daughters around.

95

Jesse was an intelligent woman, so…

"Why do you do that?" I found myself asking her one day.

"Because men need to feel like men," Jesse replied.

"I can understand that, but don't you find it degrading?"

"Look, when I play that game, there is one thing I am after. Sex! A big, brawny man does not want a woman, in most cases, to be smarter than he is. If he thinks I am smarter, he becomes intimidated, and I get nothing. I am just as apt to use him as much as he thinks he is about to use me. What he doesn't realize is that I'm a player in the game, too. A game he will end up losing. I can assure you, I will not be the one who calls a day or two later. Now, the man I marry, if I marry, will have to be able to stimulate me out of bed as much as in bed, if not more. As of yet, I have not found a man who could do both," she said.

Until that moment, I had never imagined Jesse had given her conquests much thought. I had been wrong.

"Well, I have to say I am surprised."

The truth was that I was also relieved. Jesse's confession was almost a confirmation, a tacit agreement, of the game I was playing; even if she didn't know I was playing one. It also left no further doubt in my mind about the role she would play in the lives of the girls, Ty and Sebastian. She ceased to be the constant flirt, and established a new reputation with me. If Jesse ever had to come up against either of them, Ty or Sebastian, I was sure she would be able to convince one of them, probably Ty, to see things her way. Suddenly, I was confident she would do just that, especially when going against Sebastian. Poor Ty would always be the swing vote, and, although Sebastian may not like it initially, he, too, would eventually come around. Sebastian will be angry and feel as if I didn't trust him, but he could be made to listen to reason. It would take some convincing, but it could be done.

Telling Jesse was the only way to secure the last promise. I had refused to allow her along the journey of the illness. Surely she could see the need for a woman's presence at the end of my journey and the beginning of the girls'. Her role was far more important to me when I was gone than on the road.

"I hope you will continue to honor your promise of secrecy," I began.

"Of course," Jesse replied.

"Jesse, I haven't been completely honest with you. My medical condition is much more serious than I've let you believe."

"How much more serious?" she asked.

"I am afraid there is no recovery. I am dying."

For the second time in what seemed only a few months, Jesse was speechless. As I delivered the last line, I could see the color leave her face. Then she stood and walked towards the window for several minutes, still in silence.

Without honestly trying, I'd wounded my best friend more deeply than I ever imagined possible. She only had one questioned in response.

"Why?" she asked.

"What do you mean 'why'?"

"Why did you choose to hide this from me?" she asked again.

"Jesse, there are many reason," I tried to say.

"Give me one good one, please," she interrupted.

The silence in those few moments before I replied were like nothing I'd ever encountered. One moment, you could have heard a feather hit the floor; the next, I felt as if an ant had been crawling across the floor, each step as loud as thunder. Soon after, I realized it wasn't thunder I was hearing, but the sound of my heart beating, reverberating in my ears, each beat shaking me. I felt as if I was being rocked in and out of consciousness. I needed a few seconds to gather my thoughts again, and the ability to speak.

"As I said, there are many reasons. But the most important was I didn't want or need pity from any of you. I've seen that look before, and I wouldn't have been able to stand it, much less do the things I needed to do with you all looking at me that way. I know it was selfish of me, but this was the easiest way for me. After all, I am the one who is dying."

I barely finished before she answered.

"And what about those of us who happen to love you? You're damn right it was selfish. I've never known you do anything so selfish. You denied me the chance to be there. You denied me the opportunity to help. You denied me the right to prepare. Instead, you spring this on me and just expect me to accept it and move on. Who else have you kept in the dark? Does Sebastian know?" Jesse asked.

"He found out a few days ago."

"Found out? You mean to tell me you have kept us all in the dark since that first episode?" she asked angrily.

No words were needed for a response. I simply looked up at her, and she knew the answer.

"I don't know how to begin to forgive you! A voice inside me says I shouldn't, and another says what's done is done," Jesse finally said.

"You're right. The time for reproach has come and gone. I realize I've shut you out of many opportunities to be the supportive friend. But there are still things you can do, and that will need to be done. There are other ways you can help me now. Primarily, your role as godparent will be crucial. My will is very specific as to how the girls should be educated and such. Make sure they are carried out to the letter. But, if in any instance there is a doubt, you can be the voice of reason. Sebastian will need the advice of a woman from time to time. Second, be there for the important dates: graduations, birthdays, funerals, and weddings. I know it sounds crazy, but maybe Anna and Carina will know I'm there if you are there. And lastly, promise me you won't allow the two of them to screw up my daughters' lives by being men."

I knew Jesse wouldn't let me down.

Chapter 6

The request

Treasured moments didn't come easy after my diagnosis. However, I was about to have one. This was the moment I'd been waiting for. My verbal sparring with Sebastian had been child's play compared to what I was about to attempt. Ty was much more complex, many more layers to him. He also had nothing to lose.

Sebastian might have revealed his true feelings if he'd chosen to continue to argue about Ty. I might have lost a great deal more. With Ty, I'd have to keep up, as well as not get taken in. I wasn't concerned with having an answer for every question he might pose; my main objective was to lead the conversation. My hope was to get him on the defensive, and then steer him into a corner. Somehow, I was ready.

Why?

I wasn't sure. For several days before, I'd been too weak to even think about what was happening to me. I supposed the weakness was a combination of additional medicine and general fatigue. Whatever it was, I felt unbalanced. My mind had drifted in and out of what was real, and what I'd realized later on was a dreamlike state. I knew the hospital was real, for instance, but I'd played out conversations from the past in my mind as if they had taken place while in the hospital.

However, I woke up with a clarity I hadn't had in a long while. The first thing I did was to call Sebastian and asked him to bring the girls to see me. Then I casually mentioned Ty. Was he still in Krefeld? Would he read some pages from his book? I wasn't sure what I'd actually said. Nor did it matter. Something had to be done to make sure Ty would come. Guilt had been a marvelous tool to work with. Who'd deny a dying woman anything?

The funny thing was that I'd done nothing in preparation. Most of what I needed had come from Ty himself. I had read the book initially to find out how he felt about Sebastian. However, I'd learned so much more. I was able to figure out how he might have dealt with conflict. He'd written about it with such detail. Each of his characters had expressed how they felt and what they thought. So maybe I could emulate a thing or two from them. He and his characters were one, after all, no? All I had to do was remember one of the exchanges he'd written about, and act accordingly. With a little luck and some of my own personal touches, perhaps I could pull it off.

There were things I knew I couldn't do. For instance, I couldn't go fishing with Ty like I had done with Sebastian. Ty would have seen right through that. What I had to do was state facts and get him to come to the same conclusions. Then I had to make some general observations that were logical. Once that had been done, I'd have to give him a personal reason he could relate to. Here, I couldn't lie. I had to give him something that was unique to me; something he wouldn't have been able to imagine me saying.

There was only one reason that was not a lie and uniquely personal: the truth.

Not just the bit and pieces I'd recently parceled out. The diagnosis was nothing compared to the information I saved just for this occasion. Something I could blind side Ty with and make him vulnerable, in the hopes that I could draw a confession from him. If I didn't want to see Sebastian with another woman, surely Ty didn't.

Hopefully, this would get the wheels turning in his head about a possible future, a future he'd seen trampled on once before when I married Sebastian, and, most importantly to get Ty to say the words I needed to hear.

However, would Ty see it that way? We both knew Sebastian had changed. We also knew there was no one else for Sebastian. What Ty didn't know was that I knew about their past.

However, even armed with this information, I could fail.

The worst thing I could have done was to be put on the defensive, like I'd planned for him, and fall into my own trap. To divulge what I'd learned too soon would have been a regrettable mistake. A mistake that could ruin everything I'd planned.

The determination to win at all costs was the driving force pulling me forward. I wasn't above cheating; I'd already crossed that line. There was only one flaw with this part of my plan. There was no contingency with Ty. The answer had to be 'yes', or everything went to hell; it had to be a complete surrender on his part.

Tipping my hand was out of the question. I had to hold on to the pawn of information. In my mind, it was the only one left.

Then I again, I wondered, would it have been so bad if Ty knew that I knew about his past with my husband? What could Ty do, tell Sebastian?

Would it really have been a mistake?

Would there be fall out? If so, I had to believe it would be minimal. Neither of them would be able to say no to me then; about anything, for that matter. The revelation of the secret that had kept them together for years would be just the thing to get them on the same page rather quickly. The possibilities were promising.

The questions were only debated for a moment, however. I was probably right in my reasoning, but being right was not what I wanted. I wanted Ty and Sebastian to look after my daughters, and I couldn't lose sight of that fact. This was not the way to achieve it. I'd get what I wanted, sure, but there could be negative consequences. Perhaps it would create tension, and there would already be enough. Neither of them would be able to look one another in the eye if I told them. With all they'd have to come to terms with, I couldn't add to the difficulty. The first few days of the hiking trip were evidence of future problems.

* * *

Instead, I had to keep the secret intact for a bit longer. The secret would, eventually, give them a place to return to in the past. I'd managed to remind them for a moment or two on the hiking trip. This would be an extension of the stroll down memory lane. There was only one key change: my absence.

Anna and Carina would be the common thread to make them work hard at being polite to one another. Sebastian had it done with Ty. Ty had done it with me. For the sake of the girls, they'd have to do it again, to and for one another.

Would Ty get the ultimate prize, too?

The sad part was that they would have to figure each other out again. The two of them had changed. I wasn't sure their changes would prevent them from at least exploring the opportunity. I knew it would be much harder for Sebastian.

Would Ty have the patience to stick it out until Sebastian got it together?

I found myself saying 'who cares'. The two men were too fickle to venture to say. Once I was *gone*, I would have no more control over the situation. Not that I have had much luck recently. I'd only manipulated my husband, my best friend, and my husband's best friend to get to this point.

I'd done so without any regrets, for one simple reason: to fulfill my promise the best way I knew how. After all, I wasn't going to be around. There was only so much I could do. They would have to do some of the work if they wanted it to work out.

This was what it must be like for most athletes who have trained for years and years. The big day finally arrives, and you get to put into practice everything you've learned; perhaps a single opportunity to prove your worth to those who have so diligently trained you. Then there was me.

I wasn't an athlete, hadn't trained for years, wasn't at my peak, was neither old nor young, and I certainly had nothing to prove, but still, I was ready.

When Ty walked into the room, I wasn't sure if he was ready for me.

Tick, tock, tick, tock, tick, tock.

* * *

When I walked into the room, Beatrice looked at me with a peculiar look on her face. Could she tell I was nervous?

Nervousness wasn't what I wanted to feel. Why now? We had been on holiday before; alone for hours at a time, and never had I felt any such thing. Moreover, she had been in the hospital for a few weeks now, so that was not the reason.

Sebastian had decided the girls needed to eat something, and wanted to take them to the hospital cafeteria. I quickly volunteered to take them, but Beatrice said, "No, let Sebastian take them."

This didn't make the feeling any easier. In fact, the pit of my stomach started to churn even more.

"I'm glad we have this time alone, you and me," Beatrice started.

"So am I," I lied. "Do you need something?"

"No," she said. "But we need to talk."

"Talk?"

"About Sebastian and the girls."

"What do you mean, Beatrice?"

"You know he can't take care of the girls on his own."

"He's doing a great job since you've been in the hospital."

"I am sure he has. Ty, how long do you think that will last? Yes, he can provide for them. He will pay for school and make sure they are fed; drop them off at school from time to time, even. But I've been the parent who has been there day to day for the little things, and believe me when I say there are many. We both know someone else will have to bandage the scraped knees, videotape the school plays so Sebastian can see them, buy the birthday cakes and plan the parties. We've argued in the past about his role as a father. He tries very hard. When he's there, he's great fun with the girls. And he has cut back on his hours, to give him credit. But this would be full time with little or no support. He'll do his best initially, but it will wear him thin very soon."

"Why are you saying this to me?"

"Because I don't want another woman in my house; one reason among many."

"His parents can help out, can't they?"

"From time to time, I am sure they'll want to, but they are too old to take care of them on a daily basis. We have a housekeeper, but she wasn't hired to do that, and made it clear at the start she wouldn't," Beatrice replied.

"I sorry, but I have to ask again: why you are telling me this?"

"Anna loves you. She talks about you incessantly when you're not here. And, when you are here, she dotes on you. Do you know she's normally the first person awake to help make *your* breakfast? Not breakfast in general or for everyone, but *your* breakfast. She will be a great help to you."

Finally, it hit him. I was afraid there for a moment that Ty was going to make me say the words.

Tick, tock, tick, tock.

"Hold on here a second!"

"Just hear me out, please? Carina, on the other hand, will be a bit of work. She will take my death the hardest. But, again, Anna will help you. They both love their father, but, if you were there, I know they would be fine."

"Beatrice, I have no children and I'm not sure I could…"

"Don't be silly. It's not as if I we're talking about two kids you didn't already know. They can manage most things on their own. But they will need guidance. They will need someone to be there when they cry out in pain. You can do that. We also know Sebastian will be devastated, yet, again. Especially when the time comes for me to…" she said.

"Don't talk like that; there is still hope."

* * *

I remember laughing at hearing the words come from Ty's lips. He is not only the hopeless romantic, but the eternal optimist. Ty may not have appreciated the fact that I laughed. I knew he'd see no humor in what I was proposing. He does see how serious I am. Still, I have to make him say the words. Only then will he feel the full gravity of what I am asking.

* * *

"One of the reasons I'm asking this of you is because of your never-ending imagination and your ability to see things positively, always. Some might say a little misguided and romantic, at times, from having skimmed through your first book. However, that's not a bad thing. The most important reason is because of your friendship with Sebastian. You've been part of our lives, the girls and I, for some time now, and even more of Sebastian's. I'm not just asking this for myself, but for all of us. I know you love the children as much as you love Sebastian. You've always loved him and you always will. Who better than you? You are by far his closest friend. Who will he turn to? There's no one else I trust. Will you do this? Make my last days comfortable. Help me have peace of mind. You asked a moment ago if I needed something. I need this. I don't require an answer right away, but think about it, please?" she asked.

"You're actually asking me to give up my life in NYC, move into your house, and help your husband take care of your children? Are you sure you don't need the nurse or the doctor?"

* * *

This battle is over. Ty has said the words I needed to hear him say. He'll leave here angry, but I've started him down a road.

* * *

"I am not asking you to give up anything. I am asking you to become a permanent part of this family," she said.

"I have to say, this is not the 'talk' I'd ever imagined having with you."

"Don't act so surprised. Surely, you must have thought about what's going to happen after I'm gone."

"Well, to be honest, I was planning on asking Sebastian what he'd planned to do when the time comes. But I had in by means thought of myself as… Well, I… This isn't a good idea to even mention. This would be a disaster. There has to be another alternative."

"If there were another alternative, I wouldn't be asking you. Listen, you know him better than anyone. How long do you think he could manage on his own? Weeks, perhaps even months; sooner or later, he will need help. Meanwhile, Anna and Carina will be struggling with their emotions and who knows what else. Help me help them. As I said before, your imagination is admirable. They will need that. For too long, I've let things go the way they were between Sebastian and I, and now it's too late to think he will change. Besides, he'd hate himself if he had to stop working. And possibly even me. This is not the fault of the girls. Someone will need to be there to help them understand. It has to be you."

"Beatrice, you're wrong. It can't be me. I'm sorry, I have to go. I'll come back in a day or two."

* * *

I'm losing Ty too quickly. Maybe I shouldn't have laid it on so thick. Is there any more I can say to make Ty change his mind? Is this how it all comes to an end? I have nothing to lose at this point. The only thing left to tell is the secret. Is this the right time? I can't give up the pawn of information just yet, but I can give Ty something more to think about.

* * *

"Ty, wait! It may seem a lot, I know; the girls, the house, not to mention giving up your life in New York. Sebastian will need you again. Be there for him. Be for him what you once were," Beatrice said.

* * *

There is no mistaking the puzzled look on Ty's face. He is wondering what I am saying. Ty is restraining himself from talking, but, inside, he's begun to question just what I meant. Then he stopped. He can't allow himself to think back to Panama. Or wouldn't. That suggestion was meant to make him stay. I'd drawn blood, but fortunately, by the look on his face, it isn't a mortal wound. He simply stood there as if he had to think for a moment. What could I have been talking about flashed across his face? But he knew.

* * *

How was I to respond?
I couldn't.
I'd already said I was leaving, so I did.

* * *

He'd be back. He'd be back tomorrow. If Ty was half the man I'd come to think he was, he'd be back tomorrow. I got him to say the words. And, until Ty comes back, he won't be able to think of anything else.

* * *

When I left the hospital, I was angry. I felt as if I was being blackmailed. Beatrice knew about Sebastian and me. How she found out, I may never know, but she knew. That's why she made those somewhat veiled statement 'be for him what you once were'. How did she know? Sebastian hadn't said anything to her; I was sure of that. He hadn't dealt with what was happening in the present, much less the past or the future, for that matter.

'Be for him what you once were' sent tremors of mixed feelings through my every thought.

Once, all I had ever wanted was to recapture the feelings of a single moment and make them last for a lifetime. I have thought about it, dreamed about it, nightmares, too, agonized over it, and even written a book about it.

Could we go back?

I wasn't sure I could allow myself to feel that way about Sebastian again. For years, I had carried a torch for him. This could be the one thing to put the flame out permanently. Then what would I be left with?

Nothing!

I wasn't going to be forced into a decision. I owed Beatrice nothing. If anything, she owed me!

This guilt trip Beatrice was trying to lay on me was misplaced. If anyone should be angry, it should be me. She took Sebastian from me.

I didn't have much time to think about what Beatrice had said. Sebastian and the girls had returned from the hospital. How would I explain my sudden departure?

"What happened to you? When the girls and I came back from the cafeteria, you were gone," Sebastian asked.

"I wasn't feeling well, and I didn't want to appear weak."

"Bea said you had a lot on your mind; anything you want to share?"

"No, just something I have to sort out on my own, but thanks for asking."

"Well, if you need an ear, I have two. It would help to think about something different, anyway."

* * *

Sebastian had almost become the man I'd known before. He was so attentive to everyone since Beatrice had been admitted to the hospital. He was helping the girls with their homework, getting them dressed in the mornings, dropping them off and picking them up from school. He'd even asked me what I'd wanted to for breakfast on several occasions, and made it. This was the man I fell in love with years ago; he was tender again.

It was good to see him doing as much as he was. I was happy to see brief images of my old friend again.

Could Beatrice have been wrong?

I'd never known Sebastian to fail at anything he tried. Beatrice did know him better when it came to being a father, and, according to her, he'd never been a full-time dad. Would he be able to handle this job indefinitely? Would he be able to give up his job for a life of domestic tranquility? I didn't know why I'd even allowed myself to think of such a question. The answer was no.

Beatrice was wrong when she implied this was her fault. No one could have predicted this would happen. She was right about Sebastian feeling tied down, however; resentment would soon follow.

Besides, tying Sebastian down to the home front was about as practical as trying to keep a wild pig for a pet, indoors. He was meant to roam the world and be the 'nature boy' I affectionately called him while we were traveling. Just like wild pigs belonged in the forests. As I looked at Sebastian across the table, I was beginning to understand some of what Beatrice was thinking. There was no other alternative.

Sebastian could find help with a babysitter; a sitter was not what Anna and Carina needed. They needed someone they'd already been familiar with, or at least someone who'd be around for a longer period than one of Sebastian's road trips. Most of what Beatrice had said was making sense. I began to think about her words more seriously for the first time. What *was* Sebastian going to do? Had he made any arrangements already?

Well, I needed to take advantage of the rare mood Sebastian was in to ask a few questions. Maybe his response could help me sort out some of the things Beatrice had said. I needed Sebastian's answers to either verify or negate my thoughts, as well. So far, Beatrice had been dead on about what she was thinking.

"Can I ask you what you plan to do with the girls, you know, when it's time?" I asked. Sebastian didn't look at me, but he stopped cutting carrots and looked off into the distance. "I thought we were talking about you. In all honesty, I haven't given it much thought. Bea has always been the one to take care of the things where the girls have been concerned," he said.

"I figured as much."

This time, Sebastian looked at me, but said nothing.

Silence was a new language between us. It was odd to find each other with nothing to say when we were backpacking around Central America. In those days, we'd had less weight in our lives. Time, jobs, and people had given us new thoughts, feelings, and emotions. This was something we had to work out. This new language was not written. There were no experiences to draw from to guide us on how we felt. Nevertheless, we did feel something.

"I'll stay and help you find someone if you like," I said.

"That would be nice, but I think I can handle it for the interim," Sebastian said.

"And when you can't?"

"Then I'll call someone."

"Who?"

I could see Sebastian was getting agitated at my pressing him for answers. There were few occasions when I saw him angry; a new one was about to happen.

"As I said, I haven't really given it much thought. What do you want from me? And why is everyone in such a rush for that day to come?" Sebastian asked.

"No one is in a rush. I think we would all sleep better if some things were done in advance instead of waiting, including Beatrice," I said.

"Yeah, well, doing it in advance makes the inevitable more real, and I'm just not ready."

"And doing it when she passes is going to make it easier? Besides, this isn't about you."

"Don't you think I know that? I'm not ready; is that so hard to believe? Neither are the girls. I know my own children well enough to know that. But having a stranger in the house isn't the right idea, either," Sebastian finally yelled.

Sebastian's frustration had taken hold of him tighter than a vice grip. The pain on his face wasn't hard to see. The tears were close. One was shining at the bottom of his eyelid. I could tell he was resigned not to shed one until the appropriate time.

"I'm sorry," Sebastian said.

We were in the kitchen, and the table separated us. I wanted to walk over and hold him, but, without looking in my direction, Sebastian got up and walked away.

We didn't speak to each other the remainder of the day. I left the house to think about what I was going to do. I hadn't planned it, but I went back to the hospital. I couldn't wait much longer. My flight was leaving in a few days. However, before I gave Beatrice my answer, I had a few questions.

* * *

"You're back sooner than I'd expected," Beatrice said.

"My plane leaves the day after tomorrow," I said.

"So, have you decided what you are going to do?"

"I have a few questions," I replied. "First, how can you be sure this is going to work?"

"I'm not. There are no guarantees in life; you know that."

"Exactly, so why should I go along with this nonsense?"

"Because I understand my husband, and so do you, or you wouldn't be here again so soon. I also know Sebastian will feel as if he has failed somehow. What he doesn't know is… I failed him."

"Then why not tell him that?"

"You'll have to tell him. Otherwise, it won't work."

"Why is that?" I asked.

"Because you'd tell the story much better. You are not completely unbiased, but less so than I."

"Unbiased about what?"

Beatrice turned her head and didn't respond. Was there more?

"You asked your questions, now let me ask you one."

"I hadn't realized we were keeping score. I'm sorry; that was uncalled for. Go ahead."

When Beatrice looked at me this time, I was startled. This wasn't the kind and gentle woman I'd known. I thought she was about to cry. Tears were hardly what were on her face. Determination had replaced any of my ideas of emotional weakness.

* * *

More blood was required, and, this time, the wound had to be deep. No more superficial cuts; I needed to get Ty's full attention.

* * *

"What happened in Turkey?" Beatrice asked.

My head dropped. I couldn't look at her. She knew much more than I'd imagined. Suddenly, I did have something to feel guilty about. How could she have known I was in

Turkey? The trip was a coincidence, a happy one for me, but a coincidence nonetheless. Deflection was the only course of action.

"Oh, Bea. Are you sure-?" I started.

"Yes, damn it!"

Why is this important now? If she wants to know the truth, I'll tell her. I'll still be able to keep my word to Sebastian if I tell her parts of the conversation, certainly not all. "I told Sebastian several things on that trip. The first was that I told him several of the characters in my books were based on him. He'd said he'd never read any of my books, and I got angry."

"You two drifted apart after that trip. I find it hard to believe it was over something so simple. Ty, you don't have to do this any longer. I know you love Sebastian more than you're telling me. Something more happened, didn't it?"

Why was Beatrice pushing me to go back to the one place I've wanted to forget since it happened?

"I was envious he'd found you. Beatrice, I'd never met another man like him. I told him he was the benchmark from which I'd judged all other men in my life. And then I told him about Frank. At the time, things were getting serious between us, and I wanted him to be the first to know."

"I suppose you would have nothing to gain by lying to me now."

"No, I wouldn't. I've loved your husband and my friend for years. I have also respected the fact that he is your husband first and my friend second. Nothing can change that. And I have too much invested in your family to risk losing any of you. You're the closest thing to a family of my own I'll probably ever know."

"This whole time, I wrestled with one thought for months. You came first; you still come first, in so many ways," Beatrice continued.

"I don't follow. What do you mean?"

What more could Beatrice possibly know? I'd already said more than I should have. Any more, and I would be crossing the line between the truth and my promise to Sebastian.

"Panama," she said.

"Panama; what does that have do with anything?"

"Everything! I've read *Our Orchid*."

"Well, at least one of you did. But I still don't follow what the book has to do with now. Oh, I see. Do you think you've learned something 'more' about Sebastian, me and the characters?"

"What do you think? Of course there was something to learn. It wasn't a big stretch of the imagination to know who the characters were. The hard part was reconciling what I'd been told and what was real."

"Are you asking me or telling me you know more?"

"Now is not the time to be a writer. This is no longer fiction we are dealing with, or characters that you have invented. Lives will be changed irrevocably from this point forward, and you and I need to be brutally honest with one another if this is going to work. So, shall we continue to play the childish game of hide and seek?"

What was I going to do? I promised Sebastian I would never mention Turkey to Beatrice, but she knew. Now she was asking me about *Our Orchid* as if she read my notes while I was writing it. As if she'd somehow been there. Who did I lie to from this point on: Sebastian, Beatrice or myself?

"No, there wasn't anything more. I used my notes from years ago, while we were traveling in…"

"Panama; that, I know. I have only one more question, one I should have asked weeks ago and was afraid of the answer. Every time he left on a trip, I wondered if he would be secretly meeting someone. It was foolish, I know. Now, I simply don't care. I need to know, no matter what the consequences. Have you ever been with him since?"

Costa Rica was the setting of the book. How did Beatrice know the real trip was Panama, or was she guessing? I'd changed as much as I could to make the story credible, but I had to keep it Central America. There was only one other person besides myself who knew that. I was sure Sebastian hadn't told her. The choice to lie was easy, now.

"No."

"Well, thank you for your candor."

"Candor? Now who's playing hide and seek? You've known all along, haven't you? You knew before I came here today that the setting in the book wasn't Costa Rica."

"Yes."

"So, what? This was a test of some sort? To see if I'd lie to you?"

"Not a test, no. But I needed you to tell me the truth. I, then, in turn can tell you the truth."

"And what truth is that? You think you know me? You know nothing. I've stood by and watched your life with the greatest of envy. You married the man I've loved for more than ten years. I saw the way he looked at you in New York, and I knew then it was over between us. Then, when you got pregnant with Anna, I wrote you both off for a while. I didn't think there would ever be room for me again. I thought I had to close the chapter for good when I went to Turkey. I wasn't a hundred percent sure Sebastian would be there. I knew he would if he could, so I booked a flight. When I saw how he responded to my news about Frank, I knew it wasn't over. I knew then, no matter what Sebastian may have said to the contrary, he still loved me; maybe not as much as I loved him, but something was there. The smallest flame was still lit on my torch."

"Ty, you don't…" Beatrice tried to say.

"Please," I interrupted. "Let me finish. As I said, I would never have interfered, but I wasn't about to give up. I knew it was wrong to hope that we could be an 'us' again. A part of me always held out for a chance, a moment, to tell him I still loved him. And, like you, I knew Sebastian would never leave his family. All the while you and I were kept at arm's length; that was probably more my doing than anyone else's. You had him, and I could only watch. Watch and wait. When I got the first invitation to visit, I couldn't say no. For a long time, I felt as if I had been forgotten. It was such a little thing in retrospect, but it meant a lot to me. A window was opened. Then other invitations came along, and I was all too keen to be a part of your family. If this was the only way I could be a part of Sebastian's life, I was going to take it. And, soon enough, I began to love the girls, too. Anna was always my biggest fan. In her eyes, I could do no wrong. Even if I couldn't get all of you to love me, she would. Was that part of your plan, too? Was that brutal enough for you?"

"No, I had no way of knowing Anna would have taken to you like she did. And yes, that's what I needed to hear from you. You see, I've never wanted the one thing you were determined to show me. Pity! From the minute you walked in earlier, you've looked at me like a wounded animal. Well, I'm not. I left that woman behind months ago."

Beatrice was struggling to get out of bed, and I moved to help. She held up her hand and stopped me before I could reach her.

"You're still doing it. Has it not occurred to you yet, in all that I've said, there was something missing? Some small part you haven't figured out. Well, perhaps not small. But how I know so much?"

113

"Of course it's cross my mind!"

"Good. I will satisfy your curiosity, then. You see, this has been a game for me for some time now. You were the wild card. I didn't know how you'd react to what I'd done. I needed to hear that anger in your voice. It was essential. There's something you have to hear first. It wasn't my intention to hurt anyone, and, fortunately, no one was. But I had my reasons. The only one who I felt 'owed' me anything was my husband. The rest of you were casualties of war. The end result was all that mattered."

"What end result are you talking about?"

"I cannot say that what I did and how I did it should be justified. I wasn't even sure it had to be. Maybe part of it was a bit selfish, or even childish in some ways. All I knew to be true is my girls needed someone other than their father to help raise them, and the options were limited at the time. And the way things were going, while I was sick, no one could have done better. Perhaps that was just my point of view; reality had been altered in so many ways. But things looked desperate for us all; more for me than for others. My emotions were going in every direction. I was selfish, as I said."

"Why do I get the feeling we aren't talking about the same thing?"

"Because we aren't!"

"What are you talking about, then?"

"Now, I have something to confess: I've known about Panama for a while. Sebastian was on one of his trips, and I was alone in the house. You have to understand, I wasn't in my right mind; I became more than irrational. Anyway, I got worked up one day thinking he was having an affair. Then I found a locked drawer in his study. I jumped to all the wrong conclusions. I used the locked drawer to convince myself he was hiding something. I found six leather-bound journals. For a moment, I hesitated before reading them, and then decided we have no secrets. But I was wrong."

"Sebastian wrote about me while we were in Panama?"

"Yes."

"I thought he was documenting the landscape. I'd never even dreamed he was writing about anything else."

* * *

A ray of sunlight pierced through the gray clouds. Ty's words were nothing compared to what he must have been thinking Sebastian might have written. Once again, I'd struck a nerve that I hadn't been aiming for. The reaction from Ty was much more promising than anything I could have produced. It won't matter what I say from here on out. He'll never be able to get past the fact Sebastian had written about him.

* * *

"This was also around the time I was actually diagnosed; the hiking trip was used to tell the both of you about my diagnosis. I had kept this secret from him, so why shouldn't he have kept something from me? So, I read them."

That was certainly more than I could have ever imagined. I was dumfounded. I had to sit before I fell. Beatrice read my book and Sebastian's journals, and was able to form a complete picture of the two of us. For years, I'd failed to reconcile the facts and fiction. Beatrice had done it in a matter of months.

Part of me wanted to judge, and part of me wanted to know more. What else had she done? What exactly was in those journals? What Beatrice had just told me was more than a simple confession. These were the words of a dying woman. However, I couldn't help feeling she was also making me an accomplice to her betrayal.

"And I finally understood how deeply the divorce of his parents affected him. You were there; you must have seen it, too. That's when I realized Sebastian wouldn't leave his family. He would have stayed until the girls left home, and maybe even after that; who knows? " she said.

"Yes, I was there. And yes, I saw it."

"When I was diagnosed, I pushed him away even further. The girls were mine then, not his. Every minute of every day was spent making sure they were protected. Then I found the journals. Getting the two of you back together was my way of saying I was sorry *and* taking care of the girls. I don't think he would believe me now, anyway. Don't you see? If you tell him and if you help him, it will all be made right. And everyone will get what they want in the end," she said.

Would everyone get what they wanted? The words reverberated in my ears for what seemed like hours. What did I want? What did Sebastian want? Then I had to ask myself if it really mattered what either of us wanted.

"That's why you made me so angry just now? But you must have been angry, too. Beatrice, were you angry?"

"I wasn't able to get terribly angry. Besides, I had no right. I'd lived with my diagnosis for a year before it was common knowledge. Jesse didn't even know the truth until much later. And I couldn't betray Sebastian's trust and tell him I'd read his journals. It didn't seem fair. I had a choice: I could confront the past and make everyone even more miserable, or I could have a short and peaceful future. I chose to deal with the future, or what little future I still had. The past was gone, and there was nothing that could be done, anyway. The past and the foreseeable future had to be reconciled in a matter of days, and I had the upper hand because I knew both. Sebastian didn't have the same luxury. The inevitable future was much more important. So I set about manipulating all of our lives: yours, mine, Sebastian's, Jesse's and the children's future. At first, it was just a game. It made me feel like the chess master leading my opponents around the board. I moved from table to table making moves to bring about the sequence of events that lead to the last few months."

"You've been planning this for months? And I walked right into your trap. You must be very proud of yourself. "

"The plan had been set in motion long before the holiday. The accident I had wasn't an accident. When the two of you arrived at ER, the doctor would then inform you both; all of it was planned, because I had not told Sebastian the truth months before. You had to be there to share the knowledge, to witness his reaction. I knew, knowing how you felt for him, it would make you more malleable from that point on. I also knew that, because you seemed to be there from the beginning, Sebastian would turn to you to talk about his feelings; besides me, you're the only one he trusts. The girls would have you to comfort them while I was in the hospital. A kind of prelude to what I had hoped you would agree to become at some time in the future."

"Am I the only one who thinks this is crazy? You're right about many things, but you've forgotten someone else. Sebastian. How do you think he's going to react when he learns what you have done?"

"It will take time, but I know he will come back to you. Just be there for him. Be there for the girls. Show Sebastian you love them, and he will love you. In many ways, he has always loved you: once, almost as intimate as a lover; for years, as a friend. Now it's your turn to be his muse, as he has been yours. Show him how to take care of the girls, show him how to love you again. For me, show him that a partner isn't always selfish."

I didn't fool myself into thinking that what Beatrice was offering me would not include further problems; I was a realist, after all. Fiction may have been my life's work, but most of it had been based on reality.

"You realize I'd be a fool to even consider it."

"Lover, friend or muse; which is it going to be? Could you continue to settle for one? Believe you could be two and do nothing? Or live the reality of all three? I have done a great deal of planning to make all this happen. And I am not willing to let it all go down the drain because one piece doesn't fit. You were the hardest part of the puzzle to figure out, the unknown variable. But, as long as Sebastian was involved, I had a better chance at manipulating you, too. Forgive me, but I had to do it."

"Forgive you? You make it sound as if I have no choice. You aren't asking me anything. You haven't even considered the possibility I'd say no, have you?"

"No."

"Why?"

"Because I know what it's like to feel the love of my husband. For a time, I was the center of Sebastian's world, I felt like no other woman. He made it easy to love and be loved in return. He made you feel special, protected and needed. What more could one ask for? But then I changed all that for both of us. I was the one who took that love away by being me. I don't blame him for the change in our relationship. You see, he never really changed. Regardless of what I had done, he continued to love me. A little less, I thought, but he still loved me. I was the one who took the girls away from him. I wanted to protect then so much that I forgot what it was like to have him there. He may not know the ins and outs, the day-to-day things, but no one will protect them more. He will you need you for the day-to-day things. And because…"

"There's still more? Beatrice, I am not sure I can take…"

"The longing you must have felt can now come to an end."

"Or does it begin again, just in the same house?"

"You have suffered long enough; you have loved Sebastian longer than all of us. In this way, I give him what he had once. And I do believe he will love you again. I know you still love him. I've seen the way you look at him. The tenderness in your gaze, I once held for him. You feel happy in his presence, I know. And, in return, you want only to make him happy. So, you go in that way, making each other happy."

"Getting someone else to do the deed again?"

"I deserve that, I suppose. Listen, Ty, without you there to show Sebastian what I've done, he won't come around on his own. But, if you are there, if you know everything, it will be easier for him to confide in you. And with confidence comes trust, with trust… love. A lack of confidence drove us apart. But that was my fault. You can show him he can trust and love again. Like me, you now know all the dirty little secrets. It has to be you; he won't trust anyone else. You're Sebastian's best friend. Sometimes, I think you're his only true friend. The two of you have shared more than we ever could," she'd replied.

If I were to do this, it would have to be for the girls. Sebastian had to be an afterthought. As Beatrice said, nothing was guaranteed, and Sebastian wasn't preparing for the worst. I had to get off the fence.

"I came with the intention of telling you 'no'. But I can't now. I see the sacrifice in you I made years ago. And my dream might still come true. Who could have known it would happen like this? I also know this won't be easy for your daughters. I lost a parent when I was around their ages. No reason or explanation; no one there to help me get through the change. I'll help your daughters, and perhaps find some for myself in the process. My initial thought when you told me what you'd done was that you were trying to make me an accomplice of some sort. I'm still not convinced otherwise. And, in some ways, I quite possibly could be. Whatever we decide here today, it really only affects one person, doesn't it? We both know Sebastian has a hard time asking for help."

"Thank you."

"Let's you and I be clear about something, however. I love Sebastian. But I'm not doing this for him. Hell, I keep telling myself I am not even doing it for myself."

"Then why are you doing it?" Beatrice asked.

"I can't imagine what you must have gone through to come to this decision. But it's obvious you love your daughters more than anything. And, although I won't technically be a parent, Anna and Carina deserve more. You deserve more. I think you underestimate Sebastian, however. I think he could do it. But you're right; not without help. And, as you said, it should be someone familiar. I'll stay as long as I am needed. But understand this: I am doing this to help."

* * *

Ty said he's doing it for the girls. It sounded *so very gallant. But I* felt *something different. The hopeless romantic had begun to see it like I'd seen it. Time was what they needed to sort themselves out. I'll be giving Sebastian and Ty what I couldn't give myself: time and a second chance.*

* * *

Tick.

Tock.

The queen has fallen.

mein Schätzchen=my little darling